ESPECIALLY
THE BAD THINGS

ESPECIALLY THE BAD THINGS

Greg Gerke

ThisIsSplice.co.uk

For Tess and Lily

Contents

The Wrong Things List

There were many things he did wrong in the relationship, though calling her *cold-hearted slag* and ripping the picture of them at Niagara Falls were not part of the many, but more an assertion of his masculinity—through admittedly feminine means. Yet if some people knew how she behaved, they would applaud him for his assertion, as some weeks she bordered on psychotic and she needed to see the image of them torn to activate the reverse traumatization effect he'd read about in a men's magazine. The *slag* wasn't planned, but he'd thought for a good week about dubbing her *cold-hearted*—even writing a paper weighing the advantages and disadvantages of such a coronation. Unlike his other documents, he single-spaced and justified the lines of the paper to make the arguments and ideas more uniform and official-looking, concluding he should add *slag* to demystify the *cold-hearted* breach and keep her somewhat attracted to him because of the smart words he used.

The wrong things list did exist, though he'd spent little time with it. Written on a grocery receipt in ballpoint pen, it remained inside a physical chemistry textbook he kept in a storage compartment on the outskirts of town. Some Saturdays he went into this poorly lit, chicken-wired den and sat on a box, working his mind around the points he'd made in a more fragile and delicate moment, a moment that perplexed him far more than the many things enumerated. He considered himself aloof, but not aloof from his real wants and desires; yet, if he was so in touch with himself, why didn't more fragile and delicate moments occur in his life? These thoughts often led him into less promising territory and wrecked his brow, making it look like he'd had frontal brain surgery at a hospital where they didn't care about pretty.

All he could remember about writing the wrong things list was that he'd needed to drink a large glass of orange juice before starting. The panacea of citrus, pulp, and vitamin C bucked his huddled mind, prompting a brief recap of his short existence—the swinging boyhood legs which, once he began a career in nonfiction, lay stinking on various couches like strangled pythons.

In the list itself, he referred to her as P, though her name began with L. Why the subterfuge? His father had been big into precaution too. A rustic but dispirited man who carried two green eyes that stayed alert against any unwholesomeness at his expense. Sitting in the storage compartment, he waved to his father in heaven, but smarting at the memory of how much money his father had left his second wife, his wave became the finger.

P was mentioned in many entries on the wrong things list and this worried him. Did he think she caused many of the wrong things he eventually carried out? If so, this list was actually P's wrong things list—she had authored the compendium. No. This was his wrong things list, and the overwhelming amount of P minutiae only typified her dominant nature when it came to him, though what else could she be when they'd lived greatly intertwined for five years, including a month in Peru, out of each other's sight only on bathroom breaks. Did Peru make an appearance on the wrong things list? Yes. Toward the end of their vacation she insisted on hiking one more mile, and during that mile he broke his leg and they stayed a week longer than they wanted and missed the National Book Awards ceremony he'd strategically intended to attend with a wonderful tan and a wonderfully tanned woman.

But this Peruvian moment was written as *P gives into J's* (again an alias, his name began with T) *demands for another mile.*

He wanted to puzzle out the truth, but first dealt with his annoyance at the use of present tense. Most of the list was in past tense except this episode and a few others. Did this mean the follies lived on eternally? That they were the more important wrong things? The next present tense entry stated: *J gives P the Brahms Requiem CD.* How the hell did that get on the list? It wasn't even in the same neighborhood as breaking a leg in Peru. And she'd said she loved Brahms—he remembered that very clearly. They'd just come out of the performing arts center and she'd said, I really love Brahms. She had this unmatchable smile on her face, like she was happy for all people, not just herself. They kissed and, though it was late, walked near the dangerous park because the experience of all that music and all those instruments played at the right time had set a fire in them.

As they walked into their apartment, she said again, I really love Brahms, though she reveled in symbols and malapropism, often saying one thing when she meant another and sometimes he understood her, and that night he did surmise he was who she really loved, even though Brahms added a good deal to the feeling— what else was classical music good for if not seduction?

Then they made love in the hallway. It had been a while since they'd made love in the hallway, and he remarked to himself he should sweep more often so their skin wouldn't get punctured by the small street pebbles their shoes sometimes brought in. The presentation of the Brahms Requiem CD came later in the week, maybe Thursday, almost four full days after the concert and hallway love. What happened in almost four full days? They went to work. They came home at night. Hot June weather. *J gives P the Brahms Requiem CD,* meaning the wrong thing was a result of the giving. The gift generated the wrong thing, but that ripe, orange-juice-filled authorial body declaimed the giving as the wrong thing, not, seemingly, anything in its aftermath. Did the creation called J have orange juice running through his blood at the time of gift-giving too? Yet, J was much more T as he composed the wrong things list and P was much more L when she said she really loved Brahms, because sometimes that was as close as L came to her heart, at least according to J and T. So *J gives P the Brahms Requiem CD* is clearly on the wrong list, the wrong wrong things list. Is that acceptable? How many other mistakes are there? But what about orange juice consciousness? Could he really succeed in fighting such an overwhelming force on a cold, rainy, mysterious Saturday? The giving was an attempt at something, however fearful and misguided the giver was at the time. So J gave P the wrong Brahms. P wanted T. Shouldn't T have seen that? Hadn't being next to her smell so long made an impression?

Why should he answer these questions? Why should he find himself alone as Saturday becomes Sunday? He's been alone before—after being born his mother had to leave the room at some point. If one day he isn't happy, the next could be different. He carries the same identity into each. He had the same identity when living with L—has he changed so much now that he only lives with memories of her?

Will he edit this list to come off as more favorable, as less paranoid? Possibly. Who is watching him here? No-one. Who cares about what he is doing? No-one. Then why is he doing this?

AUTUMN'S DISJECTA

Manhattan

one

A STORM CAME INTO FOCUS over the city, something characteristic of the cold mocking spring that had delivered itself only two weeks earlier. But it cut west at Stuyvesant High School and bore for Jersey City. The few drops fallen only activated the street garbage to shed odors it held while the cold had reigned.

They were sitting in the café with the cheapest products and the ugliest decor—something just above plywood encased by silver trim, chairs with cushions the color of vomit—things no single person could live amongst, things only an appeal-to-all edict from corporate could conjure.

He was her acquaintance, someone who knew her brother back in Tuscon. He remembered her from the old subdivision. Blonde now, not taller but filled out, holding a glazed plumpness the city would shave off in a few months of running about after her destiny. Somewhere she'd meet a woman who would coax her into wearing other things, ensembles that didn't mark her as a member of a college team clique—if you wore black here, you wore black with etiquette, a black that went well with a sharp knife in hand, as the vamps from film noir. Women had pressure and presence then, now they had pecs. Still, she was luscious, mainly because of her Arizonian entablature. Her mind wasn't jagged with rent worries, or the specters of bedbugs or leering, toothless men on the subway. It was cylindrical and crypto-Buddhist with a splash of liberal leanings, rightly oxygenated; her arms still expected bannisters to support her wherever she walked—ha, welcome to hard times. The mind controlled the body, or so this half-handsome man, beveled with early eye lines, believed. He'd read it on his phone and some old idiot at a bar in Carroll Gardens told him as well. The old idiot probably wanted to sleep with him, but the codger wilted after his advances were rebuffed, so his advice smelled true. At the café, his mind controlled his body, and his mind told him if he told her, You have beautiful eyes—and he would say it—she would loosen herself to him because of his positive vibe on top of the built-in trust of being her brother's friend. Even in this shitty café, they were making love already.

She smiled to give the impression of being impressed, but was she? Did she fool herself in his company? She was a little taken in and her understories pulled to please for fear of the lonely life. What else did she have? A computer, a good winter coat. Back home, her often angry cat stewed. Mom said Fred wouldn't eat and then he attacked the flat screen when the Miss America was on, and she was like, What the hell, cat? I can't hold your hand through everything. You've got to get by on your own. It's not like you have to come up with a job and figure out the silly subway. You wake up, you get fed, and you get to look out the window for twelve hours, see the birdies, eat a fly, maybe dad crinkles up a piece of paper for you to bat around until you decide, This is stupid, old man. Jesus. I mean, I can't stress about these little things. My cat, Fred? He's not a part of my resumé. I don't want to work in a coffee shop—How can I help you today? No, like maybe grow your own coffee or at least grind it. Environmentalists holding their paper cups every morning. I can spell *thermos*, can they? Man, I've got to take it easy. He's cute—does he know he cut his neck shaving? And why did that guy in Union Square tell me the Beatle who wrote 'All You Need is Love' and 'Give Peace a Chance' was a wife-beater? Why do they have to be instigating? Keep your negativity local, everyone's fighting a hard battle.

This guy, he's probably just doing the best he can—what else can he do? One of millions. Am I smiling? Do I really mean my smile? Answer the question, you jerk.

Manhattan

two

SOME BLOCKS TO THE WEST in Hell's Kitchen, a man born in Florida sat under a scaffold hemming a ritzy apartment building. Cardboard, a *rosé* box broken down and folded, kept his body from the cold cement. A serge coat he'd found in a church basement covered him. He wouldn't have said *stolen*, but he didn't recount much anymore to living people. He knew the truth and no-one else not associated with his past needed to. His black boots were similarly gifted, but, hardly new so many months ago, they were now busted and the backs of his toes had been filed into a coarse, rope-like material from poking through and touching the city streets repeatedly. They also had fifty-cent-piece-sized holes in the arches. These breakdowns kept him from walking at times, but he'd long ago decided he'd walked enough—once going most of the way from the Mexican border to Monterey on foot. He couldn't catalogue his blue jeans or the sleeping bag smeared with road tar. It had warmed him through the winter and brought him to the doorstep of April. It had his smell or he had its—a question only for forensics.

His smell was wherever he was and he was his smell more than anything—a mixture of piss, pus, creosote, scalp, sperm, lint, pits, ass. All of which amounted to a cocktail served as his most complex and best feature—even a black bear would go bounding away from it. But his body was all he had. Long ago he'd curtailed the ache to bottle, label, and subsequently drink his pee. His body changed then, his mind too—self-sufficiency can fuck over man's humane impulses. But at least he respected life enough not to kill or kill himself. Sixty-some years and he could still breathe: not bothering to bitch, not cognizant enough to worry (except short prayers about weather); not loved, loving, or expected to love back. If truly beheld by citizens, they'd see all seasons in him, all that is mercurial and saturnine adding up to a zero point—un-accommodated man. Because his penis rose nightly he averred he could produce, but it rose not at the unmasking of a body or intimacy with one he once liked to look at. It was a gradient of some miasma he couldn't conceive or at least a reaction against the cold, blood pooling to create another extension of warmth, or something representative of the urge to spray out what he drank—that of a regal diet preferring soda over water, espresso over coffee.

The scaffold had a leak and he felt the side of his left leg getting unreasonably wet. He pulled himself up and swung over, cuddling the fat blue metal tube though a large bolt bit into his ribcage—wetness always worse than pain.

Someone had been speaking to him for the last few minutes and he kept nodding his head in silence, opening his mouth in a stab at an answer, but surrounded by a forest of silvery salty hair no-one could see it. For years, he hadn't either. Maybe his tongue had lost its color along with its musculature, moving from side to side like a slug he didn't recognize. Maybe—he couldn't feel it. The person had a high voice, but he believed it to be a man, though he hadn't looked closely. They were certainly talking to him about him, but what could he add as counter? The subject held no interest. He never asked for money but sometimes woke up showered in singles, fives, and the odd twenty. Most times there were bags of food, often leftovers from restaurants, specifically pastas with rich sauces from the plethora of Italian establishments in the neighborhood. It tasted the same, same as his mother made growing up. The same as two wives made—and even no better than the Safeway brands once tasted; stuff hardened, oversalted, and coagulated, that stuck to one's teeth, even if only ninety minutes from scratch.

The man who stood before him stopped talking and he knew he could look up because he could feel when someone's eyes left him. He was someone in uniform but not the ubiquitous doorman, rather someone who had other things to do, but stopped out of some feeling, not obligation. A great angst in those clean hands that wrung themselves.

He wished to be monkish in the face of kindness, but such sanctity could clog his rectum, which had recently begun working properly after a few harrowing years. He had nothing to say—weren't there monks like that? Anything the stranger could offer couldn't help the person who really needed help and a person with nothing can only give a lesson. He couldn't tell him that his caring was kind but misplaced—some monks would say that. Should he bring his palms together? The fresh-faced man required a sign or else he wouldn't leave—or worse, he'd call the City. He raised a hand. When the young man turned on his way from one of his fussy involutions, going at squirrel speed from phone to reality to phone and back, gesticulating to someone who couldn't see him, he saw that real hand down there and seemed to understand its deeper meanings, even the cautionary, *Stop*. The young man soon said goodbye and the man's eyes cantered to the ground in reflex where a few dollars were held together by a paperclip.

Manhattan

three

AT NINE THAT SAME EVENING, on the top floor of a three-story brownstone in Brooklyn Heights, a forty-five-year-old woman finished her second high impact session of ab exercises for the day. Her trunk had the same mottle as a crocodile's knobby head—most of the vessels, veins, and other lines wiring her stuck out so she resembled a part of the Bodies exhibit. If only she had been around in 1653 and Sir Thomas Browne had performed an anatomy lesson on her, much about the female propensity to adapt and go muscular might have been deciphered without the claptrap of a little over three hundred years of beauty registering as thick skin packed with fatty meat calories.

You're so cruelllll, she sang unaccompanied against the digital recording as she stepped in front of the bathroom mirror to inspect her bulbous front. Her 1500cc breast implants would never shrink even though her body had contracted at a rapid rate for the four years of her muscle fitness regiment on top of twelve more years of high aerobics, on top of four given to childbearing, on top of nine in high school track and field and collegiate swimming. After a supplement, she took a picture, but remembered she had already posted one after the first session that glorious morning turned cruddy by what a Weather Channel flunky called the final whiskers of Old Man Winter. She didn't want any of her stalkers or former boyfriends on Fuckface to think she'd fallen too much in love with herself and what she could accomplish, how she could be forty-five with balloon breasts and possibly the best female abs in Brooklyn—not bad for a Seattle girl who married the right man and now had multiple bank accounts, each with well over seven figures. And what about those two sons? The second, Lane Jr., completing his first year at Harvard Business and the first, David Scott, working his way on the crew of the highest-rated contender for the America's Cup. Such a full life and with no body fat and no guilt the few days a week when she ate six squares of Godiva chocolate. She should reward herself for the new creature she developed into—someone who might freeze menopause and create her own hormonal imbalance—that befitting a blonde woman's outrageous sex drive, rounded by a clitoris which might have been mistaken for a smallish male proboscis. Her husband could never hope to be enough to please, especially when he worked until after nine most nights, a practice their society took for granted. The man currently in stress at Deutsche Bank really only liked her for photo-ops and the gauche, expensive, sleeveless and backless, and belly-displaying dresses she wiggled around in for her shot at *cause célèbre*, the envy of all those poor old pumpkins he worked with. Her husband liked fine meats, rich cheeses, and richer desserts, and his beer gut had never nakedly met his wife's six pack since a few days after September 11th. Rubenesque secretaries at work were his speed, but golf had become more important than fucking, and making more and more money—nothing could break down that yen. Besides, the boys needed their parents to be together, to know mommy loved daddy and daddy loved mommy, and why not? They had invested so much money in them, while sheltering them from the world, shitty as it was for most everyone else. The word *spoiled* never crossed their palates' clefts, yet still they admitted the boys retained a childhood type of neediness.

She had her own network of people to absorb her nympho-mania, including domineering orgasms, high-wire oral calisthenics (she did tongue yoga), and a penchant for playing the 5'7" Amazon—fuck the height, she had all else, and a husky voice, care of the roids, made to give orders. Young men, old men, African men, but a cop, a painter, and a neurologist were her main buddies curr-ently. She had what she described as a love-like affinity for them all equally, although the painter knew how to be aloof best, hence wetting her the most.

Opening a bottle of mango Yin/Yang, the in energy drink, she sat on their ten thousand dollar couch and began to comb her fingernails over her abs in figure-eight motions, humming a new song by a British pop tart about being lifted by her beau to new all-world ecstasies. Then she scrolled though Fuckface, but nothing important had happened, just a plane crash in Mexico. She sang some more, then thought of her dead mother before cradling her abs. What would they do with the Big Sur house? Or the one in Barcelona? She didn't like how Spaniards looked at her—like it was her fault they felt the way they did about how her body was—her people were much better at hiding envy. A person has a right to be any way they want to be. That is what she'd learned over her years—you grasp life, you work hard, and there is success. The power to get anything. Hers was so full, look at her body and her boys. She touched herself and then brought out her pump, to make it bigger. Growing it felt so good. She turned on more music in her head and thought, If I videoed this, people would pay to see it.

The Big Woman

In childhood, the big woman would sometimes sneak up on me when no-one was around. Approaching a tractor's weight, she wore smelly, ragged bandages about her ankles and a green scarf made out of a plastic kite. She never got into her name and rarely sounded at all. She always came from behind my eyes and would paste my head to her belly.

She liked me. I was seven. I smelled pretty good. I had no stubble or debt, a healthy relationship with Santa and the Easter Bunny. She just liked me. She wanted me all to herself. She cried when she had to leave.

My mother caught a whiff of her a few times but ignored the offal and had me cut coupons. I thought it best never to ask her about the big woman, but somebody had to explain. Once when mother went to buy vanilla extract, I called the Fifth Precinct. The policeman wasn't amused. You little turd! You don't call women big. They get mad if you do. They take things away. They make it difficult to watch football. If you don't get to the flower shop before kickoff, you're screwed.

From then on, I stayed clear of the phone. Instead, I called radiothons in my bed about the big woman, but the little guys in my head didn't have any answers either.

The big woman liked to bring me crackers. She carried a thimble of peanut butter and we sat in my yard chewing and licking. Then smacking, picking, and stinking. She brought a banded bundle of travel brochures and maps, and sometimes she opened them and I saw the squiggly lines she had traced from city to city. The map of the Western states, my favorite. California, a mess of ink. Arizona, somewhat. Oregon, yes. Idaho, Colorado, Utah, too, but Nevada was blank. I slammed my fingers onto it and said, Why? She pulled the map away. She kissed the top of my head with a medicinal grunt, worked her heft upright, and trudged west to the hilly cemetery. The splayed grass where she sat slowly rose—once restored, our secrets were concealed.

When the big woman left I started staining things. I thought it was what she would have wanted. I took out couches, chairs, coats, rugs, bookcases, bags of potatoes; I reached for my poison, balsamic vinegar, and stained. You see, the big woman had given me something I didn't know existed, and now that it didn't exist again I was a rage-filled, punitive American in a miniature blue-jean jacket.

When I convinced myself my mother knew where the big woman had gone, I stained her. The old man took me upstairs. Some would call it a lesson. I called it a massacre and screamed that they would never again be in my love light.

I saw the big woman once more. Her bags were just as full of newspaper and cans. She stood behind a fire truck with her eyes closed, the empty thimble dangling from her fanny pack. Features squeezed, her face glistened—it told of wrung feelings and betrayed solutions. The old man hauled me in a direction I didn't know and wouldn't have preferred. I wanted to find my hand clutching her warmth no matter if it smooched one of her steaming lesions, but the old man pulled us into an alley. To keep her bulky after-image, I tried not to blink. I held out for a while, but then we had lunch. In the chewing I remembered who I was, the parents, the house, my room—playtime. That disappeared her.

I asked the old man about the future, toys and such, but he didn't want to talk about it; he wanted to get home and see the game.

Chrissy Likes
the Dolphins

She kept it hidden for a while and then sprang it on a night when we started to have sex but didn't finish. She pushed my thigh off her thigh, cleared her throat, and said, Ted, I want you to know, I like the dolphins.

I nodded and went to the bathroom. I didn't think she spoke about dolphins in general and she'd never mentioned football as an interest, but we'd only been married a year.

The next morning I found a Miami Dolphins pennant on the refrigerator, and at night Chrissy came to bed in a droopy Dolphins jersey, the bottoms of the two numerals at her ass. I sat in the dark for a long time. Will the Dolphins be good for us? I asked.

In the next week I awoke three times to her watching games from the 1984 AFC Championship season. Her hair in pigtails, her pom-poms orange and blue. Jesus Christ, I said. We have to go to work in two hours.

She twisted a pom-pom in my face. You are fair-weather. So, so, so fair-weather.

At the office I staggered around, staring at other, normal-seeming women. I spoke to Leslie about good dentists in the area. I joked with Madeline about file folders. Problems on the home front? my supervisor asked.

Well, Chrissy really likes the Dolphins.

At home I was made a dummy that Chrissy practiced clipping penalties on. She salivated as she said, It hardly gets called, but when it does, it's totally awesome. She went to her reception job in close to full regalia—no shoulder pads but strapped and cupped. In a few days she was fired and immediately urged a move to Miami. I snapped my fingers in front of her nose. I like Cleveland and you said you like it too.

I told friends, I told family. I told our neighbors. I told everyone. They would not reply. I went to the police and they laughed. The Dolphins weren't even in the same division as the Browns; what the fuck did they care.

I looked around my city, wondering about the world and how my sexual needs related to it. We hadn't done it since *The Coming of the Dolphins,* as I now referred to it.

On a Sunday when Chrissy had the four Dolphins fans in the area over to watch the game, I went to a bar with no TVs, a red interior, and a reputation for bringing together people's genitals. I found a woman who wrote werewolf novels. She'd lived in Scotland and had straight black hair and three-inch fingernails. She knew I was married; she knew my kind of problems. I went after her large hands but she swatted at me with her latest werewolf manuscript. I don't think this is going to work, she said.

But you know me, I cried. You know the issues. The wife that becomes another person. You write about it all the time.

I write from the viewpoint of the werewolf, she said as she wiggled out of the booth and stood up. She must have been six-foot-seven. I could understand her then—a really tall woman wants a really tall man. I bemoaned my lack of inches and she slapped me. And don't tell a woman she knows you, she said. Then she whacked me again. And that's for the werewolves.

Denise, Dogs,
and Me

DENISE WAS UPSET that Cheryl had signed the petition to make Brooklyn more dog-friendly. Why are you so mad about it? I asked her. Because Cheryl signed the petition only because her boyfriend Keith lives in Brooklyn, she told me. What do you have against Brooklyn? She had nothing against Brooklyn and she was okay with dogs too. It was the principle. But why is that your business? I asked.

You don't understand, she said, and she started to describe mistakes I'd made in my life. Some I didn't remember, some untrue. She said I'd had the affair with the jazz guitarist out of spite for jazz. You see, Denise laughed, you do the same things I do— only you get better results. You silly photographer, you—there's something about the way you work or how your mom bounced you. And she always felt a little uneasy around me because I borrowed money from people and pretended I didn't know what they were talking about when they came to collect. You're puerile, she said, adding that my pictures of the peninsula were barren, existing not only out of reality, but out of the realm of the beautiful, and really, what was my point?

And you talk to me about a dog petition? she said.

I didn't even like dogs, so Denise spoke more truth than she could possibly know. But railing on my peninsula pictures couldn't be forgiven. I rented a semi and carefully wheeled it into Denise's

Queens neighborhood, only clipping a decade-old Honda on the way. I played with the airbrakes until she came out of her gray house.

Hi Denise, I said. I've decided to run over your house with a semi today. She didn't say anything, just walked to the front tire and kicked it.

I wanted her to remove valuables. She returned to the house and cranked the TV.

Maybe I wasn't a good photographer, but the maul of machinery into a pre-war two-story made up for all that. I killed a lot during the first run-through and then I killed some more. I slapped the semi's door like she was my horse.

I Might Be Here
in February

AFTERNOONS I WALK MYSELF to the window of the Rose and Thistle. Young, unemployed people cavort there. They laugh and flirt. They drink. I look down at the layers covering my shrunken breasts. If someone comfortingly inquires if I'm lost, I point to the haberdasher on the corner. Just waiting for my coat to be fixed.

Dr. Derrick Foster stopped making love to me seven years ago in June. It's an odd month. My wedding anniversary, Father's Day, the blueberry festival. Dr. Derrick. The only man since my dead husband. He wasn't so much a man as a mirth-making robot with a Jaguar. He kissed all my crow's feet before bedtime; he preached indifference. I beat insomnia by holding his ass.

Can I tell you about the day my life changed? The Rose and Thistle was undergoing renovation, so I walked into a flower shop. A group of women stood in a circle by the asters. They carried on with breathless cries, hectoring salutations—like the group my dead husband played softball with long ago. These were gathered around a child. One of the women handled my shoulder in welcome. Want to see the precious, precious?

The baby looked browbeaten, Lithuanian—he wanted something more. I scoured the store for a substitute rattle.

A woman who wasn't with the group, but who wore two sweaters and owned the shop, meandered over to me. Her aqua eyes were set apart, reptilian and relaxed. A crazy hairdo—straight from bed to work. She began talking to my shoes, Can you get them out of here? I have a titanic stomachache.

Karen was an older woman like me. I assumed she adored the Buddha because there were sixty figurines in her store. I'll try, I answered. But I'm not a lucky person. I told the women I was an arsonist and paraded an orange lighter across my lips.

Karen became my friend and soon we went to restaurants and farmers' markets, cackling about a man known for his squash, a man who had five total eyebrow hairs. Our daughters were both in college and we thought they should meet. They will get on so swell, she said. Maybe my Melissa will outgrow her bad habits. I couldn't say my daughter kept her distance from me. The blonde who adored the beach and wanted a better life, not to listen to the things I was afraid of. My dazed son remained.

I started sleeping in Karen's bed on Sundays. I'd dally there till noon, pretending I had purpose. It tickled her to leave the impoverished in the dust on Monday morning. I have to go now Maxine, she would say. I have to receive the fresh batches from this funny man who's not in good shape. His nose is always running down his coat and he tells me about the locomotives he's studied. Why do the lonely choose me?

Listening to her readying herself, I'd nuzzle her pillow and imagine a lemony scent where sheet dandruff and dead skin reigned. Her showers were long, but not hostile. The invitation was mostly open. But I liked that bed. I liked the coffee adding up in the kitchen. Karen in her beige robe could be broken and bleeding in the shower—I owned that bed.

When I chose Karen I chose frustration, yet I needed to make things right. My son had once tried to marry a stripper. I slapped him around and pretended to vomit. You don't really love me, he growled. I wanted to tell him he was wrong, but I could feel the changes taking over. Staying in, not answering—hoarding my prison's ceaseless time. He used to be more difficult, then I told him that he couldn't have any more money until I died. I sold everything and entered Karen's mess of a bungalow.

She and I continue to grow attached and worn. During the week I try to keep order in the house, but the flower business is not so kind. Karen boils sauces to explode and hides my library mysteries in her dresser. After she leaves in the morning, I laugh the wrong way round because she's awful, she's shattered. By men who were all ego. Karen pretends it isn't bad, but dirt continually spreads from her mouth. She likes to go up to strange young men and say, I've had you a bunch of times. Now I can never kiss disappointment goodbye.

We see a healthy dose of films. In the darkness, I soothe my lady's hands, nicked and cut by her flowers. Later, she tells me what I missed on the screen, what the trouble was, and how they solved it.

We go to the Rose and Thistle and sit on the patio, smiling at the street or sky. Karen has her microbrew and I have my tea and I'm the one who is cold. At first she was against matching anoraks. We aren't a bowling team, you know.

My heart, these are coping mechanisms.

I sip and sink my bag to make the taste bitterer. Then comes her petty disgust, all hairy and oily, contaminated especially for me. You know, Maxine. If, down deep inside, I was a good woman, I would have told you how much I hate that you don't work, that you don't care about your children or your skin. She yucks it a bit for the people sitting nearby and then goes to the bathroom to crumble and wash her face.

I smile at the unsmiling people. They can't know this is her way of asking me to never leave. After, in bed, I hold her tight and Karen hits. Rubs at my recent bruises and tells me I can't possibly understand her. I say, My love is easy to manufacture. I tell her

I prayed she would accept me into her life, and the wings holding our love would grow. She quietly waits until I stop touching her. Then she can sleep.

Finding and Faulting

ONE DAY A WOMAN from my animal behavior class and I went to a park and soon fell in love. She wasn't tall in the mathematical sense but appeared so because her neck was long, her hands large. Miko was born in Tokyo but grew up in Ohio, figure skating competitively until she discovered the pleasures of poli-sci. Early on I told her I couldn't skate, and she rubbed my nose and whispered a tale in Japanese that I took to mean: Even if you had no legs, I'd love you.

We became a couple who liked to take long rides in the country. Sometimes we left school early and drove winding roads into terrain pulverized by Ice Age glaciers. The prairies were wide, the sky above stretching all ways as we cuddled and cooed in a small forest abutting a farmer's field. As we held hands, we pinched our noses to block the cow dung, and each time we found a birch tree we kissed. We were at ease and so we grew.

Weeks on, though, clouds of moodiness would sometimes envelop me, especially when we went into a certain café and there was no place to sit. Standing, my thighs would shake. It didn't matter that another less populated café stood two blocks away; it was that one or nothing. In those moments, caught in the entry, unmoored, Miko would try to rub my arm or back but I would twist away, and this only made me feel worse because then we didn't have a place to sit and I didn't have her touch. If I didn't have one, I couldn't have the other. I felt scared and a little lonely. I thought if I could just explain my state of mind to Miko during these curious, cruel moments she might forgive me and never leave.

I saw the situation as me being in debt to Miko. Though she probably would've understood an English explanation well enough, I decided to fashion one in Japanese. The easier I made it for her and the harder I made it for myself, the better I would feel—though a quarrelsome part of me believed by going to such trouble, I'd earned the right to act withdrawn in the future.

I visited the office of Japanese studies and soon met an American-born professor. I don't remember how I found out Professor Crestor liked pound cake, but I considered the dessert a gift for helping me construct the letter of explanation to Miko. A predilection for pound cake wasn't on her CV on the department's page or on her internet dating profile—a sweet, fatty, filling thing just seemed the best way to go.

Over the course of a few weeks we put together a fifteen-thousand-word letter of contrition. As I read my sorrowful lines out loud in English, Professor Crestor, short with a slanty, unsmiling mouth, would nibble on the pound cake and fidget with the CD player in her office. She preferred piano music, but only liked certain pieces on her many piano music CDs, often having to eject the CD after only one or two pieces played from a possible fifteen.

We could have finished the document sooner, but Professor Crestor wanted to tell me about her ex-husband and how brilliant he was. Apparently he'd been an astronaut, but one who never made it out of the control center. I asked how he could have been considered an astronaut if he never went into space, but she ignored this and told me how in the fall she'd travel to Germany and present a paper on the role of the tea ceremony in Japanese culture and how she used to love Berlin more than she did now, which reminded her how much more she also used to love Tokyo.

Where did they go? she asked, and answered herself, I can't say, as she stared at the dark books lining her office.

Luckily Professor Crestor was unlike Miko and not very attracted to or interested in me. If they were similar she might have tried to interject some secret commentary into the letter warning Miko about how I shouldn't be trusted, especially since I bought the cheapest pound cake in town. Where Miko was calm and graceful, Professor Crestor was loud and awkward. Flitting about her office, she often tripped on her Persian rug and swore in both English and Japanese, sometimes German. Whereas Miko never cried, Professor Crestor would sob as she composed the symbols of my sentiments. When I first thought it was the sad piano music that made her break, and attempted to power off the CD player, she swatted my hand and told me the sad piano music kept her from crying more. I've had a different life, she said, while lighting a cigarette with pale, shaky hands. But I still like to help people. I still like to see others succeed, though it's funny that you love a Japanese woman yet won't attempt to learn her language—but that's me. Compared to you I'm a different person. I used to be thinner. Teachers sit many hours of the day.

My few weeks with Professor Crestor made me cherish Miko more than ever. After sharing space for more tortuous hours, I walked through the university cemetery, my eyes leaking. How could I have treated my lovely Miko like I had when there were Professor Crestors in the world? And what if I became a male version of Professor Crestor? Had I already? I knelt down by a Dwight Vogel who died in 1965. It could have been anyone down there but I felt close to Dwight in a way I couldn't explain. He was different from Professor Crestor, even from Miko. He didn't judge, he didn't say anything—just remained.

On the sly I began to compose a companion document in English for Miko. It described Professor Crestor and all her foibles and how my exposure to her had altered the light in my eyes. I told of wicked conversations that made my stomach burn. I detailed the way she mashed her cigarettes into a white marble ashtray, twisting and pressing with guttural moans until the butts were shredded fuzz, while she argued with me about the English meaning of forgiveness versus the Japanese.

I had kept what I did every Wednesday a two-hour secret because to talk of Professor Crestor without the original letter she authored might have angered Miko, though in five months I'd only seen Miko mildly upset once and only because I insisted she get drunk. Though slight, Miko could drink five bottles of sake and not lose a step. Therefore, it cost around $150 to get us both blitzed at a Japanese restaurant. Though I paid the bill she was perturbed and started kicking my shins. When she realized what she was doing she shrieked and stepped onto the first city bus she saw to disappear for the night.

The day we finished composing the letter, Professor Crestor invited me to her house for dinner. In trepidation, I countered with the idea of a Saturday lunch and she grudgingly agreed. She still wanted wine and told me which store to visit as well as the exact wine she wanted. I went to the store and bought the wine, but I couldn't enter that woman's house. I invited Miko over to my apartment and we drank a few glasses before I gave her the two letters. I was going to have her read the Japanese one first but at the last moment pulled it away and insisted she set her soul on mine.

Miko brightened when I handed her this letter and I thought for a moment the other might not be necessary. But by describing Professor Crestor pityingly, did I identify with her? Were Professor Crestor and I so much alike? Maybe we had sprung from the same emotional tree, while people like Miko were anchored higher, stronger in spirit, unbothered if the sun didn't come out for a week.

We sat on a couch by the window. I wanted to touch Miko and for her to touch me. We drank Professor Crestor's wine instead. She kept watch out the window, finding or faulting some part of the landscape. Not touch—my mind only wanted to know hers. All these thoughts curled into confusion, and I took the almost empty wine bottle and stowed it behind the couch. How could I give or give up and relax? With her in no hurry to read my letter, I offered the other and she read a paragraph or so before her head sunk.

I accepted this as sadness, proof I would soon lose my most precious human contact. But Miko, all watery eyes, refused my reading of her. She told me she knew I was sorry and the letter as a gesture was important, but not its contents.

I opened my lips to again voice my regrets, but she covered me with her small hand and asked if I was ready.

SCRIBBLERS

High On the Thigh

THE POEM HE WRITES is set in Rome, on the winding road they walked one morning to get to the park that contains the museum.

They are walking slowly because they are tired, and the poet uses plain language to describe their motion. They pass a bird pecking a baguette. Maybe this isn't even a poem, he thinks, but eventually he continues and they do as well. He's not playing it for laughs because his audience doesn't like funny poetry, and anyway the situation is serious—they go to the museum early so they can get many things done, so they can see great art on the other side of the city. As always, he carries the food and water. She isn't talking and neither is he, and that's why a poem is the correct form. His fiction is dialogue-driven because he says little in real life, and as per real life the male speaker of the poem can't answer simple questions put to him, and he begins a new stanza, inside of which the walk continues pretty much as it once unfolded in Rome. He mumbles about how good the museum is going to be and she agrees. They drink water and test their Italian on the deserted boulevard.

The poem is becoming shit, so he adds dialogue. Nice making love to you this morning, he says, and she can't say anything to this so she laughs—an odd reaction because usually she'd have a reply spinning in the air before he placed a period on his sentence. Maybe she isn't his character anymore and isn't that delightful because he's progressed in how he's able to mask real people, making them unreal and sympathetic at the same time. But she becomes very unsympathetic when the laugh collapses into a sneer, and suddenly masking isn't going too well. And it's just how she'd laugh—very underhandedly, thoughtlessness ripe and swelling, as sometimes, truly, she didn't have to say anything. Yet those times were less memorable for him because she didn't use words or she laughed at a low volume, but being the author of the poem he can see and hear everything, and he kind of understands why he left the relationship—it's better to see and hear everything even if it's bad since at least it won't be hidden.

The poem then loses its distinction as shit and the male speaker of the poem asks why she is laughing and why won't she use words to answer him? As he's had direct experience with the woman alongside him, the poet answers, saying she laughs because she knows how things will turn out. Even in Rome where they are seemingly loving with each other—traces blue-black, high on the thigh, though covered, exist. The speaker of the poem asks the poet if they can go into the museum and have a fun time and not do anything else except go back to the hotel and make love, but the poet is ambivalent because that's not what happened. He knows they saw great art, that she touched St. Teresa's toe, and that he became enraged and asked her to please not touch the great art and she didn't laugh and told him to go to hell. No, no lovemaking at the hotel.

You son of a bitch, the speaker of the poem calls the poet and the poet chuckles because they have the same mother, and he proceeds to write the speaker of the poem out of the poem so the voice is more distanced, more how the poet sounds after being away from her for a year, being away from Rome for two. The boulevard is still deserted and, given the male character in the poem couldn't make morning love, being so eager to see great art, he decides to let the sun come out. The character is lost and overwhelmed by a city he will never see again and she grows more sympathetic, but when presented with St. Teresa's toe she's still going to touch it and that's probably good for the poem and the poet, because the poet needs to have something outrageous occur and he's glad for her, happy she kept her outrageousness, at least through Rome. Initially it's what drew him to her and allowed him to show her his early sketches and manuscripts, though it's what he eventually couldn't stand and had to get away from because in the end life is serious and death more so—that's why he favors poetry, because it's august and melancholic and people go *Mmmmm* after he or someone else reads a good one.

This exercise has gone well. And in what better place than Rome? And what better than those two lovers filling that place? What better than him defending her from the guards? What better than this colossal lie, this poem?

Zoo Ending

WHEN HE PICTURES the end of the story, he sees it end at the zoo. The characters: a single father, his daughter, and the nanny the father hired. The little girl sees the elephants and runs toward them. The father wants to smoke, but there's the issue of the heart murmur and he's uptight about dying. The nanny beside him is shorter, bolder, and more sure of herself. She wants to wrestle the story away from the worried father and even from the seven-year-old who hasn't had a single break all story until the elephants. In someone else's hands it might have become the little girl's story but she has a lot to learn. He thinks her smiling satisfactorily while feeding the elephants won't go over. The child is not changing, the adults are—and adults are the ones who read his work. Quickly, he directs the little girl to run toward the lion house and that's the last the reader hears of her.

He stops the pen and considers the nanny. She's sort of young, sort of sympathetic—she enjoys life. She's been a good nanny and she doesn't have a lot of money. She is right to wrestle the story away from that worrywart who secretively drinks. Also, women read more fiction than men, so it's appealing for the woman to have the last laugh. Maybe she'll reject the father sexually and still be a mother to his daughter. Then she will be free to roam and fantasize and eventually attract a certain type of refined man to complete her life—very akin to the author himself, he thinks. A man who sees the beauty in mothers, the supreme life-giving force that he has so embraced by dating mother after mother, until his last relationship with a woman who wasn't a mother yet fancied herself one.

Was that the problem? No, it was more along the lines of her criticizing him and him writing science fiction to make money and stop the criticizing. But after one story sold and the criticism didn't stop, he looked at his life and saw waste in himself and rot in her. He left her, leaving everything, even his writing desk, and moved into a friend's house, thinking of the woman he held onto for so long and loved—that woman who was not a mother, but who could have been and even could have been the mother of his children. Who was she really? These are questions he thought he'd left behind, but he always carries them into the next piece, sci-fi or not. The way he tried to solve the problem of her was by creating another woman, a young nanny free and attractive, and now a mother, though her body never experienced the rigors— motherless children need mothers. The nanny feels kinship with the little girl—the nanny truly wants to give her the puppy she desires. He decides everything is perfect because the nanny char- acter loves him, the writer, in an affirming way his former love could not. The hair color is black, not brown. She does not criticize, though she wants to be center stage, which he allows because she is so selfless—so bold, yet composed. She does not cry all the time, but is strong and not resentful. Soon, the little girl will be very taken by her new mother and will shrug off the early, mis- managed rearing of her inattentive father.

He ends it there. *No-one can touch her*—the nanny, in her new freedom. Is that the last line? It feels right and sitting on his friend's couch for the last four hours, trying to figure out the end, he decides he can't wait any longer for a better one, his coccyx really hurts. But a while later, he feels he should give the reader a small promise of just how happy this odd triad could be and changes the last line to, *No-one could touch them.* And in the middle of the night, coughing and feeling unwise and powerless in a strange room on a couch not meant for sleeping, he changes it to, *No-one can touch him.*

Overtone

HE HAD JUST BROKEN UP with her and felt free, yet horny. Felt kind of happy, yet replete—though he didn't know what replete meant and he'd left her the dictionary.

Then he began reading a novel about a woman who has a tough time when a relationships ends, so tough that she lurks around trying to find the man in the city where they live. Ha, he thought, what a sad sort. I'm so on top of things—I'm losing weight, I'm watching baseball again, and I don't even worry about being made fun of for posting a picture of my angry cat online.

As he continued the novel, he found it bizarre he would keep reading about a human being at odds with herself, but he wanted to see if the couple got back together. They didn't and he was pleased, because in real life people don't so often get back together. But the novel wasn't real and the woman inside it was so desolate at the end, so crushed. After closing the book, he felt a false sense of happiness.

The author was a good one. She'd won prizes, she'd been translated in Africa, and she'd made him complicit in this woman's debacle. He walked around his favorite park wondering if a mistake had been made. He'd broken up with her, yet he felt lost. He wasn't supposed to feel the way he was feeling, and beyond *lost*, he couldn't describe it in his own words. But the woman author certainly could. She was smarter than him, more successful, and she lived alone in a house on the Pacific Ocean.

Goddamn her, he shouted. Goddamn her so much.

Here Is the Poem

HERE IS THE POEM. It's called 'At the Fishhouses.'

Here is the rock they sat on as he read the poem to her. It's a man-made rock the city towed in as a barrier to the sea.

Here is the man. He's not a poet, but he writes essays about poetry.

Here is the woman. She's taking a bath and thinks about whether she should continue wearing baseball caps in public.

'At the Fishhouses' is a good poem. It takes up three pages. Little rhyme, but repetition and repetitions built from a sad time of living. Cold dark deep and absolutely clear—he quotes for the nine-hundredth time. What does that mean? He can't just keep writing essays about Elizabeth Bishop. He coughs because otherwise he'd laugh and he doesn't want to laugh because he's in a library. He starts another letter to her. Opening line: *I fell out of love with you a long time ago.*

To her credit she remembers the poet. She has to—living with a man obsessed. But she remembers the poem as 'The Fish,' not 'At the Fishhouses.' I don't care if you've caught a tremendous fish, Ms. Bishop—I went to Dartmouth. She'll never see him again, never open another letter. Never call his mother to ask her how her leg is doing. The woman has daughters for that, a sensitive-ass son. She wants a son and wants him to look like Cary Grant or at least be sophisticated and half-foreign. But what if he gets hooked on steroids? His bones would ache, his hands burning up. Steroids and treating women like dogshit. If she couldn't have that happen to him, how could she ever have him? She's sick of questions and blows a bubble. She never liked sitting on rocks anyway—that magazine article warned of haemorrhoids.

It's the best opening line he's ever written. It's certainly better than *Tush!* What was Shakespeare thinking? She's never going to be able to put this one down. Instant classic—though that's an oxymoron, but so what? He's the teacher; he can make the rules! Except when it comes to her. Troubling. Once he controlled her and now he controls nothing. What should the second line be in the most devastating letter he's ever written to another human?

She pushes the water and finds memories. Chokecherries at her grandmother's house. What a grandmother, and what a house. She wants that house, but does the house want her? She lathers her elbows. It wasn't really wrong of her to be in a relationship with him. He knew many things; he knew why the Thirty Years' War started and the names of all the teeth. Big deal. Her feet are dirty and she runs the bar between her toes like a saw. It feels nice and she saws into hurt and the spaces glow clean, then bloody, and she thinks, This is my poem, cocksucker. Stay out of my tub.

To ease off and make her think he might have access to some psychological sense, he tries softer notions in the second line, sett-ling on: *This is not to say you don't have a few good qualities.* But then he goes a little berserk because Bishop would never slip such a sentence into one of her letters. She wouldn't shirk poeticism and play in a sandbox of cliché. But when did this become about Bishop? It's the unseen woman he has to deal with. The woman who broke the glue. Bishop and her fat nouns and verbs will always be on the page for him. A pushover, her. Turn and push over her. Abandon her for the abandoner—the one who shaves her legs on Tuesdays, the one who claimed her judgments got clouded from too much gluten.

Walking on heels and moaning, she flies onto her new bed and the expensive lime-green comforter billows out. Blood slinks to her ankles, tickling stickiness. I'm so happy, she breathes into her mind. Blood in bed, blood on tongue. She leans over the side and looks for any hairs that may have fallen from his head. None, but the bed smells new, even fungible. He is the man I loved.

The letter ends at one line and he scurries through the stacks hungry for a river. Through the heavy doors he finds only clouds. They are bright but not clear. They don't finish a story.

She lies in bed, cold. New or not, it's all the same. The hour dark. Deep inside, her fingers pluck. She forecasts more breath and lets herself act how she was destined to act. In heat, with many cries and a heart timed not to flower.

Storied

She wouldn't let him do what he wanted to do and this frustrated him. She was a painter and he was a writer and he tried to read his stories to her, but she would stop him and tell him not now. With others he wouldn't give in, but she was older and he thought she knew better. It pained him not to share what he wanted to share and he thought it odd how he truly desired this woman who deprived him of doing what he wanted to do with her.

He read that run-on sentence again. What exactly was odd about his behavior? Wasn't that how relationships worked? In the past, yes. But he had been writing for some time and seeing women for some time—he had gotten to the point where he wanted something different from his writing and from seeing women. Writing it so it would happen, he wrote that as they walked into her purple-walled apartment he announced he wanted something different and she said how admirable that was, but she still didn't want to hear his stories.

He then asked to see her paintings, but she said that was not a good idea, and he became enticed because there was something she had that she wouldn't show him. Because she was a painter and he had not seen her work he couldn't tell people he was seeing a painter because he couldn't answer questions about her work. What was the attraction of her being a painter then? Maybe she lied. Maybe she made beaded necklaces. And he said, Hey, I have a story about a woman who makes beaded necklaces, and she said, What the hell are you talking about? And he said he didn't know and kissed her, and she liked that and he thought it odd she would let him do that. But odder still, kissing was actually not what he really wanted to do, though she was tall and beautiful. He stopped kissing her and asked again if he could read her his stories and she wanted to know if he was kidding and he looked at the tip of his nose and said, No, not kidding—he wanted something different. She smiled and said his something different and her something different didn't really match. He said he didn't even know she wanted something different, was she just being a copycat? She laughed and said she knew he was younger, but thought him mature enough to realize her something different could probably ensure something longer-lasting because certain mysteries would be preserved. But he protested—he was very mature because he was writing the story, he knew the entrails of her mind, what would come next, and she again dismissed being party to his art and stuck her tongue down his throat to stop any more words.

Reviewed

SHE READ HER WRITER FRIEND'S new book of flash fiction. She read to review, but being a writer, also to steal. Skipping around, smiling at a few sentences, she tapped her jaw as she identified with the sad characters. People often spoke of how similar her and her writer friend's styles were, and she thought, No shit. He'd taught her how to write—at least until she'd slept with him. Then no more talking—sex galore—but he did write poems about her breasts, cursive on weighty calligraphy paper. He was not a good poet; he sounded like Keats in a Cuisinart. And her breasts didn't resemble his physical descriptions—had that waterskiing accident really addled his memory?

After reading most of the collection, she started the review. In a cheerful tone she outlined the qualities that made her writer friend's writing thrive. Yes, the themes were riven with melancholy, but such was life, especially for writers and especially writers who didn't know themselves, who drank themselves drunk, who could express what life they had only through sex. She carefully spaced this parade of attacks throughout the text to seem fair-minded, and, given her writer friend's extraordinary impishness, she thought he would react kindly to such thoughts and would even want to start something up with her again because she was not as timid as she seemed.

She tried to write something of her own then, something wholly different from the style of herself or her writer friend, something from a coyote's point-of-view, but she stalled and called her writer friend. The call went to voicemail. She said his book was one of his best and that not once did he ever fool her. She never felt love for him, even when she had nothing else in her life—no child, no friends, no degree. Never, no love felt.

She went onto her sun porch with a drink and laughed. Now she had something to write about.

Careful

SHE TOLD HIM TO stop being so vociferous and this really upset him because he liked the word *vociferous*, liked to use it in his fiction and liked to read it aloud from his fiction, but he never used it in conversation and he would be goddamned if he let her get away with directing such a pox on him, so he flew to Europe without her and she was so pleased he had, she said in a text message he opened in Paris, and he threw the phone in the air and it landed on the roof of an apartment building. He climbed the stairs and tried to get to the roof, but an old woman appeared at the top and she started hitting him with a cane. She must have had major lean muscle mass because the blows hurt, and while he explained what he was doing in her building, she kept whacking like a crazed machine, and when he realized he was explaining in Spanish he switched to French, but ill pronunciation caused the blows to increase. Being so close to the roof door, he could hear his phone ringing—probably a call from the young, petite translator who wanted to meet with him, he'd been counting on that meeting for days, but he had to retreat because the old woman would not stop and he wondered if he had to start carrying mace and what that might mean in terms of the women's movement and the men's movement, and ultimately his sales, and he really needed a French-English dictionary because he wanted to call the old woman *vociferous* in French, he wanted revenge, but now he was on the street, the old woman guarding the front door, his phone registering missed call after missed call, and he looked at his small hands and said, Fuck me.

In Bed With Ireland

Sitting in bed, he read a short story set in Ireland, and by the end of the first page he felt he'd read it sometime before. *Shabbily dressed man*, boats, Donal—the word *jauntily*. Big into adverbs the author was, he thought.

He stopped reading and began to write another section of his memoirs. The Ireland section. He too had been shabbily dressed upon arrival, so he added that. He wrote a little diversion about a leg injury sustained. Then the nightclub scene and the following days with the Spanish woman. Still shabbily dressed at the time, they kissed in St. Stephen's Green. They kissed and argued. He pretended to be upset and so walked jauntily. He told her, I know I'm walking jauntily, but don't take it personally. She liked his face, but not his jokes. It would never work. It didn't. He stopped writing.

It was the last time he'd ever read a story about Ireland. It was the last time he'd ever read right before writing. It was the last time he'd ever read or write in bed—his back hurt. He lurched up and gingerly made his way to the medicine cabinet.

Lyrically

HE WENT TO BED in Brooklyn and dreamt his ex in Miami had published a short story in a literary journal he'd wanted to be in for years. In the dream, he stood in a Barnes & Noble in San Francisco, because he used to live in San Francisco, and opened the journal and immediately went to the bio.

He didn't read the story because his alarm went off. Dazed, he walked to work, but he wasn't really dazed. He stopped and yelled out, I'm not dazed! Dazed, he continued to walk to work. He stopped again and cried out for understanding. Because his ex-girlfriend could see he was suffering, she let him walk to work undazed, though he was disturbed, because she now wrote the story.

Maybe he had not dreamt what he dreamed and he felt a little relieved because she was just a beginning writer and would make a number of mistakes along the way. The bio was certainly all her—speaking of her man, his muscles and how the hot, happy couple smoked cigars together. He could never construct such a situation, though he had visited the experience of her with another man, and with him for hours, no talking, all eyes, all sides, back and forth, all of him going in and never coming out. She stole lines from Beckett and she didn't even know who Beckett was.

At work he turned his computer on and wondered why she wrote his thoughts so lyrically. His own writing ambled along on a few well-placed adverbs and snappy, though ultimately melodramatic, dialogue. No wonder he hadn't gotten into those big journals—he had to be lyrical like her. So, though at work, supposedly creating spreadsheets, he began to go lyrical.

Over and around his reality, he typed up dreamy texts. Ode language, angels, a sentence starting with *sinuously* and proceeding sinuously. Lyrical enough?

Not really.

Why?

He typed faster, convinced it was all him, but it came out her: *Saddish felt he. A quiet creature, his friend. Couldn't he wet his noodle and stop breathing like a tree? He'd carried him around, glowered foolish and knuckled honey to keep insane all the same.* What the fuck was he writing? Breathing like a tree? That didn't mean anything; she didn't mean anything. She'd read some Wallace Stevens in an anthology and thought she could make it new, but pound for pound she was wrong. Nobody breathes like a son of a bitching tree and, though he didn't want to, he looked at the sentences he'd composed. He read and reread and his thoughts told him it was goodish, above quality, above what he'd ever written, and he disagreed, strongly.

He liked to treat his stories minimally, make the mark miniscule. No! He wanted minimalness without the consonance, without loads of luminescent lyrical fever. No! Not *without loads of luminescent lyrical fever*, just *without lyricism*.

Let me be! he cried, callously. And he beat his head on the computer, thinking he couldn't cry callously, but there he was at his desk and the tears were callous, bricks falling from his eyes, not sweet or sorrowful, but dangerous, disarming.

Goes and Does

To AVOID WRITING, he calls a friend because she's in trouble and he needs to accomplish something. She tells him the trouble has passed and he quotes her some poetry: *I'm a martyr to a motion not my own.* Who is that? she says. And he tells her he doesn't know, though he does—he knows the book, the year of publication, and what the poet's parents did for a living. Soon enough, he names the poet.

His friend is frustrated. Why do you do things like that? Teasing. It's not teasing, he says. Well, I don't know what it is.

Ending the call, he claps his hands and walks to the window. The crusty bars of the fire escape look hideous in the high summer light. Someone should do something about that.

Still, it's so beautiful out. The birds tweet, the airplanes keep to a pattern. It all never seemed so good, except when he had it good and that was a long time ago. He thinks, When you do have it good, you don't sit around thinking how good you have it—you live the good, you live without thought. But all becomes too much thought and he goes to the Eastern philosophy section in the bookstore to try and regain the good, though he knows Buddha and Lao-Tzu wouldn't counsel such a term as *regain*—it's too late-twentieth century, too clinical, and if he were drunk he might pronounce it *Rogaine* and he quickly checks his hair, his only good feature.

So he calls the same friend and tells her the situation—it is he, trouble with him. What kind? And he says the kind that makes you think you're all alone, no-one caring, never did.

I want to hit you, she says. He'd kept blank from her, covered his heart, and why didn't he say anything before?

Putting it off, he says. He thought if another person was in enough trouble that they said something about it, then maybe his trouble wasn't too much trouble because he could hardly bring himself to talk.

What you've said means you are in the most trouble, she says.

Maybe that's why he couldn't write and he wants to tell her how confused and unloved he feels, not to mention in a creative crisis, but he scours his belly button like a cotton candy vendor and produces a leaning tower of his own nervous energy. His nose rankles, but he stares and succumbs, and though she yells for him to speak and not go away again, he already has and is silent for minutes. He writes it out: *Seeing inside his dreams, marking the days consecutively, finding pride in his pain and diving into the steam.*

He puts his pen down, tells her what he's done, and voices the lines exactly as they'd left his mind, with no edits, and she says, What steam? What dreams? And, Please come back and talk sense in my ear.

He tells her he has to go and write a little more. He goes and does, but it isn't as good as the first glimmerings—the words don't step up, they don't twin his brain like the first squirt of uncommon sludge and he decides he didn't write those first lines—it was someone from Yale or a bad translation of Rumi come to the fore, a fore rippled, but stippled, and the thread to all that is valuable falls at his feet and dances away on the floor, no kiss goodnight.

He calls his friend, but she is half-asleep. Is the trouble past? she says softly.

I don't know, he says. Tell me more.

But you keep calling me.

I'm here for you.

Twinned

WHEN SHE FINISHED writing the novel at the colony, she went for a swim. She swam with another novelist and a short story writer. Later an essayist joined the group, and he told them about his new piece on quinoa.

She left the pool and dried herself, listening to talk of quinoa. She told no-one of her novel.

Back in her room she wrote a letter to a man who stole a toucan for her. *You were <u>not</u> thinking of me when you stole a toucan,* she wrote, and laughed so the folds of her stomach rippled. *You shot it for yourself, just like I write for myself and not for you, because you aren't a reader and you think didactic has something to do with the dinosaurs.*

She poured pineapple juice into her wine glass and looked again at the last page of her novel. The concluding paragraph with descriptions of sky and surf, the light across the bay, the evening fireflies. Unholy and majestic, the protagonist said.

After juice she wrote the last paragraph of her letter to the toucan man. *In conclusion, I want to say the weather here is stunning. It has inspired me, unlike some things I saddled myself with. A pack of fireflies near the shower hut stays constant and is a treasure. I often sit at my window and watch the home of a fellow novelist. She is from Nebraska and has lived alone for the last eight years of her life. She is the happiest novelist I've ever met, and she's kind. Yesterday she hugged me in the garden and told me how my dedication to my book inspired her work on her own. Quickly I told her of how she had moved me to leave an unfulfilling relationship with a man senior only in age, and she told me not to speak of you like that, but to celebrate your good points, and I told her about the toucan. She didn't say anything, but just touched her face with a sigh.*

SOME FRIENDS

My Brooklyn
Writer Friend

MY BROOKLYN WRITER FRIEND says he's through with angry women, and I say what about me, and he says, You're not so angry, how else could I even tell you such a thing? I wouldn't risk making you angrier if you already were sufficiently angry, he says. I'm not stupid. I don't want to create angry women. Only in my fiction, he laughs.

My Brooklyn writer friend is not a good writer, because a good writer could see that I am an angry woman. The subtle hints, what they are I'm not so aware of, would leap out, but I suppose I should be happy I'm not labeled an angry woman. I might be very unhappy if I was, though I am angry and very goddamn unhappy about it.

Four years ago, I slept with my Brooklyn writer friend. We were watching a movie in my apartment. He had insisted on an action movie because he was better able to clear his creative head watching these. When it ended, he put one of his feet on my thigh. I thought only women did things like that, but I was wrong and a little angry about it. I tried to ignore his foot—a soiled, off-white sock saved my skin from his. I went into the implications, not of his foot, but of me being wrong. And I wondered why I had lived my life without ever having come across a man playing footsie. I had been to risqué parties, I had been with a man who called me Bubbie, yet no foot did he lay on his Bubbie. If only my Brooklyn writer friend knew what was brewing, what was afoot—but

I said, Oh, and then he used both feet and I grew ever angrier until he pulled me over and we started what was supposed to feel good.

Four years later my Brooklyn writer friend is no closer to publishing his novel. Two years ago, he told me his regular revisions had progressed into heavy revisions and that was the last I heard. What my Brooklyn writer friend does instead of writing is go out with women and then tell me what they were like. Though I'm unclear if these descriptions are more first impressions or haggard judgments after they've had sex.

Despite living in Brooklyn, my Brooklyn writer friend is not smart. He doesn't know that he increasingly increases the anger of an already angry woman who talks to pantyhose, and even if I were relatively lighthearted, the freewheeling and often maligned accounts of his notable affairs would create an angry woman from scratch. Additionally, his descriptions of the women he sees are poor. *Amy has long hair. Lydia acts wild*. Any good writer would know an audience, especially a female audience, would like to know the color of Amy's long hair, how Amy wears it, what Amy does to get it that way, and what, in the end, Amy's hair resembles. And describing how Lydia acted wild would be appropriate and even welcomed. Does Lydia swear at cashiers, does Lydia throw little kiddy balls to her beloved when visiting Walgreens? Maybe the name of the store is unnecessary. How about Lydia's height and weight? Astrological sign? No wonder these women are angry.

His latest is Kaylee. Kaylee's from Arkansas, he says, but this time he adds a little more. My Brooklyn writer friend is mad because she doesn't know who Kafka is, and Kaylee's upset because he didn't tell her he had a son—that he waited three weeks before speaking up. A son is an important matter, I tell him. My son is very far away and that's how his mother wants it, he says, glaring around my dark living room. You didn't seem to care.

When I go to bed I imagine my Brooklyn writer friend in a sea of angry women. We don't know one another, but we share a gargantuan hatred for this man who continues to live his life in our presence. We sit on him is what we do, not letting him free to infect with his angelic face and unadorned language. I feel a little better watching him squirm, but my anger remains.

Three Rich Women

MY NEUROLOGIST TOLD ME I'm a nervous person. She says this to many of her patients, but it's too easy. Of course we are nervous people—we have nerve problems. If she laughed after she said such a thing I might respect her. I would know she didn't take herself seriously and that she was happy to explore other ways to buy my trust.

I know all about her years in medical school and the long hours, and I feel compassion because I went out with a doctor. This doctor girlfriend constantly reminded me how many hours a week she worked and how many years she had to go before finishing her residency. I know how many years you have to go, I told her, I live with you. Then I would laugh but that was the wrong thing to do, and now I think my neurologist shouldn't laugh after she tells a patient he is a nervous person because that person might get as upset as the doctor girlfriend I lived with.

I would feel closer to my neurologist if she took me in her arms, rubbed my hair, kissed my eyes, where my nerve damage is, and refrained from speaking. Then I'd know she was something more than what I've come to expect. And I would feel right in the head, not guilty for being a nervous person.

Most of my life my eyes have been good. They were really really good years ago, when my mother told me I had to take care of them. What the fuck is she talking about? I said to myself. My eyes were fine. I wore glasses, but I didn't have any other eye problems. And a lot of people wear glasses. A lot of people wished they had glasses and some wear them even though they don't need them, thinking they look better having them on. My neurologist wears glasses and when I ask her if she really needs them, she hands me the card of a psychologist friend of hers.

I disobeyed my mother's eye advice and it turned out my mother was right, but I'm pretty sure she didn't expect to be right, so her victory stands as unearned and accidental, though every Christmas I get reminded of her triumph.

When I first had the eye trouble I wanted my doctor girlfriend to help me. She was a family medicine doctor and she examined my eye and said she didn't see anything wrong. I stared at her the rest of the night, primarily with my bad eye, thinking she might add something to the diagnosis, but she just yelled that I forgot to buy ketchup and how could she buy ketchup when she worked so many hours a week.

A few days ago I called up my doctor ex-girlfriend and told her what the neurologist said, about me being a nervous person. I wondered if that could be true, and if true, was it a bad thing?

She said it was ungodly true and as to whether it was a bad thing, it depended on how and on whom I was using my stores of nervousness. She also surmised my neurologist was probably an unhappy person since she knew many unhappy neurologists in the area, and also all doctors say weird, authoritative crap, which I should know because I lived with one. I agreed with her and she immediately became incensed. Why did you agree? she yelled. What is the matter with you? I told her my nerve problems were acting up and she told me I should probably go to another neurologist because this one clearly didn't like me and what else did I want from her, free samples?

My mother was never crazy about my doctor girlfriend and she probably wouldn't like my neurologist either. She has been right about too many things in my life, as if God showed her what

I would turn into when I was born. I really wanted my mother to like my doctor girlfriend, though more than anything I wanted my doctor girlfriend to like my mother, because by then I was living every day with my doctor girlfriend. I wanted her to like my mother so much I took them to a fancy Serbian restaurant. I even tried to order a second very expensive bottle of wine to make everything easier but my mother acted out. She said I didn't make enough money to be so extravagant. Then she looked briefly at my doctor girlfriend. After I dropped my mother off at her hotel I asked my doctor girlfriend what she thought, and she said my mother was okay, but she needed a few more glasses of wine and hadn't I ever told my mother she made only $40,000 a year as a resident.

Now I'm down to just my neurologist and we aren't likely to be intimate anytime soon. I could jump to a male neurologist. I figure he wouldn't use the nervous line because men are often less personable and more afraid of conversation, even male doctors, but this might increase my nervousness because I'd think he was keeping something from me. I look at my neurologist's bill and I see six zeros where there are only three. It's all right. I'm paying to make her happy.

They Do Not Complete Me

My Uruguayan friend is angry I've become friends with someone he used to live with, a man he grew to hate. That man also hates my Uruguayan friend, though he contends my Uruguayan friend's hatred for him predates his own. He's a more enlightened sort, he says, he never hates first.

At the café my Uruguayan friend motions to the ceiling and huffs at a woman who's knitting. His water cup is empty and he won't refill it, though he's very thirsty. I know you two share this Zen thing, he says. You do it together. You be good then.

I want to tell him Zen living is not about being good, but this will only upset him more. And it will upset me, because I don't like to talk about Zen, especially with people who dismiss it.

Why am I friends with my Uruguayan friend? Maybe we aren't friends, maybe we just like to throw a frisbee around with someone who, when asked to throw a frisbee, won't waffle and will just say, Sure.

But my Uruguayan friend has something on me and it has to do with the last woman he went out with. While we were at a party, Lucinda kept peering at me and making side comments about how I chose to sit on the host's couch rather than dance when everyone was dancing. Everyone was not dancing. Beside me was a mascara-loving woman and we debated the price of bagels. Lucinda would dance for ten seconds and then stop and stare at me with arms crossed, then dance for ten more and stop again. Finally, my Uruguayan friend's girlfriend threw a tub of ranch dip at me. I looked for my Uruguayan friend, but he was in the corner getting high.

Why are you so mad at me, Lucinda? What have I done? She said it was because she knew I had told my Uruguayan friend I didn't think so much of her. And truly, some months out of the year, she did struggle. One time, after we'd all been drinking, she smiled at me, grabbed my forearm, and pressed her long scarlet nails into my flesh. I didn't think such a person would be good for my Uruguayan friend—he was kind of sensitive and non-violent, except when it came to people he hated. But I never told my Uruguayan friend my opinion—I told a co-worker because this co-worker had just told me about a lady friend of his who went out with a guy who wasn't good for her. I wanted to say something in response because my co-worker usually gets upset if I'm quiet—he thinks he's done something wrong and that also, in certain lights, I look like his stepfather, a man he loathed. But I'm thirty years younger than your stepfather, I said. Don't argue with me, he said. So although Lucinda was wrong, she was also right—I had spilled my discouraging thoughts and she could feel it.

At the same party, my Uruguayan friend insisted he drive me home. Lucinda complained bitterly. She wanted me to ask other people for a ride, though I didn't know anyone else except the pro-price-gouging bagel lady, and she was on a bike. Why are you doing this to me? Lucinda sneered. My Uruguayan friend said, It's called friendship, and she didn't say any more.

We sit in the café and I listen to more complaints—about the time his former roommate brought out the dictionary to show him what *karma* means. This was done in front of many guests, including my Uruguayan friend's sister. What kind of person does that? he asks. And you like this guy?

I tell him I like what he represents, though I'm confused about the representation's meaning. This other man is someone I can talk to easily, more easily than I can talk to my Uruguayan friend. But he's a mess with the frisbee. We need more than one person, otherwise we will get worn out, and that's not what we want to happen.

Issues

I HAD A FEW ISSUES like crying and being mad at everyone. My friend, who lived thousands of miles from me, tried to help me. She wanted me to meet her other man friend who lived near me. In her emails she said I was a good guy. In his emails he said helping me out sounded like a good idea. In my emails I said if someone used the word *good* one more time I would break their legs or at least fuck up their email account. In a joint email they said there was no need for me to swear, that they were just trying to help me. I emailed back that maybe I didn't need their help if they weren't willing to let me act the way I wanted to, because after all I was the one in trouble. I didn't receive any emails for a while so I emailed I was just kidding and said that some people who knew me where I lived thought I was a good guy. I only received a forwarded email from my woman friend detailing cheap airline tickets to the Caribbean. I emailed back the Caribbean would not make me less angry, but I mistakenly emailed this to the airline and they happily responded, wanting to know how many tickets I wanted. I emailed back I couldn't buy tickets because I had a lot of problems and my stomach hurt. They emailed I should try peppermint tea. I emailed back the suggestion seemed very holistic on their part and my idea of what an airline was had been totally blown up. They emailed back I should never send an email to an airline containing the words *blown up*. I emailed back I was sorry, but no-one replied.

Telling

MY FRIEND ARI tells me he's going to tell me something he does not want me telling anyone. I agree and he tells me about going to a philosophical discussion on aesthetics that took place at a house in the hills. Most of the people had never met before. He says, They had pigs in blankets up there—but you can tell that part, okay?

Women and men equally in attendance. Some old, some young. Some very attractive. My friend Ari tells me there was a woman and I ask if this is the part I can't tell. No, not yet. This one woman looked younger but was actually older, just how he liked them. Her fingers were long and he guessed pianist and how did he know, she said, folding her hair before it sprung back to where it normally lay.

When a small man opened Schopenhauer to prove his own point right, the general discussion devolved. Then a woman from the Michaels Endowment made gas as she said, Must we be mean? And that you can tell, Ari says.

When a man who named his dog Adorno started yelling about platonic love, Ari motioned for the pianist to follow him out of the room. They were on opposite sides and he thought she was looking in his direction (she was but pretended not to be because everyone could see he was motioning to her) and he kept jerking his head toward the door, desperately trying to get her attention. And that's a part not to tell, Ari says.

The pianist eventually followed him to the kitchen where he suggested they walk outside, and they did. The grounds were wet from an afternoon shower, yet they moved among the apple trees and began kissing. You can tell that, Ari says, but I'm not so sure they were apple trees.

She knew how to kiss, she was older, but never let that fool you into thinking all older women can kiss well. How old are you? he asked, and I told him the figure. Well, you know what I mean. And my friend Ari decided he wanted to go to Hungary with this pianist right away, and not because she had been there many times to perform, but because he had never been and was a little afraid of traveling to foreign countries that weren't English-speaking. And that's probably another part not to tell, Ari says.

Leaning on a tree, he called an airline and bought two tickets so the pianist would know how serious he was about her. And now we are back to the things you can tell, Ari says.

And this woman, who was petite in every way except the fingers and had a leafy autumn scent about her, laughed and said how Ari was outrageous and she liked outrageous, but outrageous only to a degree and Ari smiled. He knew he had her and it felt good to come to a philosophical discussion with nothing and leave with an older woman—if Flaubert were alive he'd say the same thing. They kissed more because the kissing was of a different nature now—it was kissing with future assurance, so though a little less heated, the kissing had progressed to a satisfied stage. And be sure to tell that, Ari says.

When they came back to the philosophical discussion, the man with the dog Adorno yelled in the direction of a bookshelf, but the room smelled sweeter—potpourried. And then the discussion ended.

As their car keys jangled and people promised to keep in touch and even have lunch some week, the pianist told Ari she would be getting married in Philadelphia next weekend so Hungary might not work so well. And that you can tell, Ari says.

No, I say, you don't want me to tell that, do you?

Yes, I do. Tell them and tell everyone because I need to put someone in that seat next to me.

Babar Goes to His Friend's House and Thinks

HIS SINGLE-FATHER FRIEND reads *Babar* to his son. He sits beside the father and son thinking about the woman he's going to have later in the night.

His friend and his son are happy people and Babar is so regal, so placid. But I'm going to have so much sex tonight, he thinks, so though they are happy now, I will have future happiness. I can see my happiness coming towards me and I'll lay it and lay in it and it won't smell like elephant. We'll sleep a little while, my hand in her hair, and then we'll wake up and want each other again, and because we won't be in public there will be no games about it. One turn and that's it; there we go.

He decides he must leave a glass of water by their bed at night. If he gets up to pour it, he'll have insomnia, and she becomes very moody if he wakes her up because control can be her thing and she has to go into the bank at ten. And sometimes she says weird things about his friend and his son, like how they can't be all right without a mother in the house, and how he's probably feeding his son drugs to calm him and make him forget the absence of true family. How could such an ugly sentence come out of a face shaped so beautifully?

So he'll say to her, You're just upset because you want to have a child. I told you we could have one, but I really want to see Australia before all that starts.

And then she is silent and happiness ends because nobody has much sex after such an exchange. And since happiness has already been guillotined, he reminds her that if you don't have sex you can't have children. No, he wouldn't say that, but she imagines it was something he could say but would withhold, because he wanted to hang on to her for the sex and that makes it worse.

Then he would be on the couch, his back muscles fucked, as down the hall she cried, her throat sometimes opening and *Oh God* coming out.

After his friend puts his son to sleep, he asks the friend if he can stay the night.

My Bed-Stuy Friend

My Bed-Stuy friend insists she has a fat ass. No, I say, you don't. Yes, she says, I do. My Bed-Stuy friend is five-foot-ten and one hundred pounds. I once liked to bicycle with my Bed-Stuy friend, but since she decided she has a fat ass she's refused to ride. They will all be looking at my ass, she says. But we'll bike fast, I say. You'll bike alone.

The change in my Bed-Stuy friend predates her discovery of her own fat ass. We went to a waterpark in New Jersey and when I returned with lemonade, she was crying. A text message from Derrick had ripped her heart open. He said he still thought of her, but only when he didn't have another woman to think of.

Don't listen to him, I told her.

I didn't listen to him; it's something I read on my fucking phone.

Does that mean it's easier to dismiss?

I don't like talking to you. You're always on your own side. Then she put a towel around herself though she hadn't gotten wet. Derrick's text messages only made her eat less and worry more, and she announced there would be no waterparks in her future, no Coney Island, no Mediterranean either.

Soon my Bed-Stuy friend does not return my calls because her sister is sick, but she must have forgotten I know she doesn't have a sister. I spend two weeks talking about my Bed-Stuy friend with my therapist. I miss work. I miss my mother's birthday. I begin to look at my ass in the mirror every morning. It's getting bigger, I tell my teddy bear. And it's amazing it's getting bigger because

I'm not eating food. I can't. The penance of not eating will surely bring a halt to the non-ballooning of my Bed-Stuy friend's non-existent fat ass. It has to. I get birthday candles and fireworks to celebrate the disintegration of her fat ass, but mine only grows and I have to buy new corduroys. I call my Bed-Stuy friend to assure her all the weight she thinks exists in her ass actually has been deposited and continually grows in mine. She dubs me dumbass, but I entreat her to see it for herself and she agrees. But we can't meet in Bed-Stuy, she insists. Better in Bushwick, where no-one will recognize my fat ass. Or mine, I add.

So we meet in Bushwick and my Bed-Stuy friend is frail—she doesn't have cheeks of either variety. I plead with her, and when I steer my rump her way, a choking sound starts in her throat. I shimmy because I know my fat ass has charm. I giggle and the giggle rips my cheap-ass corduroys and I will have to go another ass size up, but I know my Bed-Stuy friend's ass will return to normal, and that's all I can ask for.

The Shirt

HE WENT TO PICK UP his good shirt from his avant-garde filmmaker friend. As he'd gone through a tough time, she'd held onto the shirt for him. She certainly didn't have to, but she did because, she said, You would do the same thing for me. So he traveled across town to find her a special gift brownie and then traveled back, arriving with blinking eyes. After a moment, his avant-garde filmmaker friend went to her closet and produced the shirt. He forgot to present the gift brownie right away, his heart already savoring the fabric in hand, and he reached into his satchel and almost said, Here's a little something for you, but changed it at the last second to, And look what the cat dragged in—equally awful, but without the nettling diminutive. He smiled and held the gift brownie aloft.

While his avant-garde filmmaker friend did like brownies, she did not like ungrateful people, or at least people who weren't grateful in time. She'd allowed him almost two complete minutes to give her a rightly deserved gift and he'd failed. Now he stood there holding the shirt to his nose, but their friendship was over and she bemoaned the fact her art took so long to produce because she wanted to make something about this character who she was once attracted to, still was, but dismissed for monetary reasons. Would he have ever held her shirt if it needed a safe place when she went through tough times? She didn't have a favored shirt, but if she did and also lost her house or her job or her print of Stan Brakhage's *Dog Star Man* and went a little cuckoo, she would not visit his expectantly sour apartment to store her many-times-laundered-in-preparation-for-separation shirt because he probably wouldn't be there. If he was there, he would probably leave his iPod on the whole time she talked so any special instructions would sound just the same as synthesized drumbeats, and if he didn't have an iPod he would have a young woman in his room who he'd recite Macbeth's *Tomorrow, and tomorrow, and tomorrow* speech to—so depressing, learn a fucking sonnet—and if he didn't fill his bed with Willy's help, then he'd have filled it by doing something daring like putting his hand on her heart and mumbling about flower petals, and that's why she was friends with him, she liked the daring of the population, they made the world go round, but were also repellent and thus wonderful subjects for film, just not avant-garde film because character was not so important there, image being everything or most things, and that was what she specialized in and she wasn't going to go narrative, no goddamn way—she was who she was and wouldn't change and they would just have to accept that. And when he left with his shirt, she repeated how they would just have to accept that. And when she smelled her closet to make sure the scent of the shirt was gone, she said she was sorry for who she was. Where had her life gone?

Bach, a Beard,
Two Women

With laptop atop lap, he stared at a picture of his friend's bearded, grinning face. In the corner of the screen an open chat window lit up and a woman messaged, *Hey, hey you.* The window beneath this window had an email from a woman he thought he could love, and playing through the laptop's speakers was *Bach for Relaxation.* But there was no relaxation with his body's brain stunned by all the connections.

His bearded friend being a new friend who lived a few states away, he told the bearded friend he liked him and liked being a new friend to him and was glad they were friends, though he couldn't yet tell him about the women he desired or his Bach-love because maybe his new friend would think he was gay to love a dead German dude and he didn't want to offend his bearded friend or Bach—as Bach could have been gay despite the twenty children. He himself was not gay and he assumed his new bearded friend wasn't despite the beard, though if he was gay they could freely talk about Bach and Bach-love.

The woman he chatted with lived on the other coast and she was a nice woman. They'd met at a Mexican restaurant and drank to forget, then drank more to remember. He'd actually brought up the chat window before he opened the email from the woman he thought he could love, but the chat woman hadn't responded to his initial prods, so he opened the romantic email because he

had some old love in him and he needed to get rid of it, and he'd
just told another friend last week that if the internet was good
for anything it was getting rid of old love. He turned up the Bach,
a solemn guitar piece reminding him of the other coast and romantic emails, but not chat windows. And just as the old love appeared
in hand, it disintegrated like snow. Guitar steady, love going—the
woman in the chat window said, *Hey, I thought you wanted to chat
with me*. Uh-oh, he said, because without the old love he doubted
any other love and clicked to close the chat window, leaving only
a picture of a bearded man and, behind that, half a romantic email
full of the beginnings and endings of sentences. Though the email
glowed ghostly, he again confronted that bearded face and relaxed
before it because this face wanted nothing or little from him and
how delicious a concept, how unlike his every experience of love.
He wanted nothing of the face, let alone the beard, all 30,784 black
hairs, and with an Ouija-like determination his mouse snapped
shut the email and left Bach and beard.

He zoomed in on the beard and saw platonic love possibilities
built on beard hair, built on the grown cheeks of a man looking
up and away, out of photograph, out of view, out of desire, and
what better? Be it Bach, be it wonder—the beard was there to
stay. Always on laptop, though located a few states away, in bed
or sopping cereal milk, it grew but didn't harbor. No psychology,
no clean living, but sprouting always, and finally he extinguished
Bach to be with beard. Beard, strange and new. He laid back with
laptop atop lap, one window open, one program running.

My Unhappy Writer Friend

MY UNHAPPY WRITER FRIEND called yesterday. Things were not improving for him. He'd sent his ex stories with female characters very similar to her. These women experience pain emotionally and physically—get wronged in every paragraph. His ex didn't respond, he told me, and he had started to fall into even deeper waters of desperation with major inarticulateness, because when he picked up his laundry and found a sock missing, he couldn't think of the word for sock and had to point at the smelly beige thing covering his ankle. They were all laughing at me, he said, and I love Latino culture, but they belly laugh big time, and from their bellies into mine their laughs infected with a fearsome ghoulishness.

That's a great description, I tell him. You should write that down.

My unhappy writer friend has been unhappy for as long as I've known him. Yet his father has to be one of the most vivacious seventy-five-year-olds in existence. Stunned to think he'd produced such a downer, I asked him in a private moment at a dinner party if he ever worried about his son, and he told me his son had made certain choices in his life. He then started to sing a song from 1946 and I understood our private moment was over. Soon my unhappy writer friend called us into the kitchen. He wanted his father's singing to stop because he'd just received a not-so-nice email, and what were we talking about in hushed voices? I can't believe people, he cried. Just once would I like— His father tried to massage his neck, but my unhappy writer friend knocked over a glass of wine and his contributor's copy of a literary magazine turned pink, and he motherfuckin'ed his father, me, the glass, the wine, Trader Joe's, the magazine, the editor, and his story—Not one of my best, they never take the goddamn good ones.

My therapist gets tired of me talking about my unhappy writer friend. She wants me to think about what it would be like to live in another city—a metaphorical city with skyscrapers and fire departments, one not counting my unhappy writer friend among its citizens. Make it metaphorical, she warns, not real, because if you moved then I couldn't see you anymore and that wouldn't be good for your head. I agree to work on visualization and after the session she tells me her husband is taking her to Ireland for three weeks. I joke about Dublin being a highly metaphorical city and she tells me to help myself to mints on my way out.

Back on streets, I open the six text messages my unhappy writer friend sent while I was in session. *I'm dying here* reads the first, third, and sixth message. The second: *I wonder if I should get into schnapps.* The fourth: *You've been very nice to me over the course of our time together.* The fifth: *Good new story about my ex. Dump truck hits her. She's in half-coma. Uses Ouija board to profess love to former meant something.*

My unhappy writer friend's birthday is usually an occasion for incredible sadness and regret, and this year is no different. It's only him and me for a while—his father comes late. Then Todd and Chloe. Chloe was in a poetry workshop he once taught and she always remembers his birthday and calls him a fine man of letters. Todd's face appears coated in white makeup. He carries a vat of peanuts and jumps whenever someone uses a sentence of more than one word. I wonder what method he would use to kill my unhappy writer friend.

After greetings, everyone is silent for three uncomfortable minutes. Then my unhappy writer friend gives a speech about his prior year on the earth and what he's learned and how he can make improvements in the one ahead. Midway through, or at what I hope is midway, his father tries to gather everyone in a circle to dance, though we're in a small studio apartment. My unhappy writer friend starts yelling how he doesn't want anyone to dance while he's talking and his father asks when he will be done talking. I don't know Dad, he says, I haven't planned this out. Then my unhappy writer friend details plans to revise his least autobiographical novel and his father laughs heartily, scooping icing off the day-old cake and into his mouth. I want you all to know, my unhappy writer friend says, how much you mean to me and how much your support supports me.

Me, I say.

What? he says.

Me, me, me, me, me.

We look at each other for a moment and I realize this is my chance and he sees it too. Warping, his skin droops and starts to smell. It's like I've hit a skunk.

Oh God, Chloe says, and he says, What are you trying to say to me? And I search the floor for my bag, but I can't find it. No smooth exit, no continuation of my sprint to freedom.

What I'm saying is—we love you too.

SUITE

The Bookcase

IN JANUARY his girlfriend inherited a nice bookcase from her Aunt Ruth. He came home from work one day, folded his ham slices into bow ties and ate while examining the bookcase. This is a quality bookcase, he said, but his mouth was full and he littered ham on the floor.

His girlfriend rejoiced over the bookcase. It looked old, like how Vienna might have once looked. He claimed to love Vienna and so she thought he would stare at the bookcase and finally let her be.

The bookcase occupied him because it was empty and it smelled like 1978 and 1978 was a good year. He was seven and eight that year. A lot of ice cream and orange soda, but he'd hated penmanship class.

Disturbed, he went to the basement for a while, but there wasn't much to look at down there. *That bookcase you like is upstairs*, a voice in his head told him and he returned to the bookcase with a bottle of Kahlua.

At midnight he made a little bed in front of the bookcase. He sang it a three-verse love song.

The Bee

THEY WERE WRONG FOR EACH OTHER, but they were in the same car. She was Norwegian and didn't make a big deal about it. He liked that, but less and less. A bee flew into the car and she laughed.

Why is she laughing in such a danger situation? he thought. I'm driving. The insurance company calls me if we crash. She gets carted around night and day, and what if I told her she's only in my presence because going to a swimming pool alone is odd? I don't want guys hitting on me.

Did she laugh thinking of their favorite shared Shakespeare quote? *The fault, dear Brutus, is not in our stars, but in ourselves.* How many more times could that be funny? She didn't even like Shakespeare—Ibsen forever! And she loathed how he carried that academic hauteur even though he said he didn't. But it's summer and I'm trying to make it work because unemployment is a bitch and the musk smell behind his ear still invites me.

The bee was in the back. It was mad because she was laughing at it. You motherfucking woman, I'm a bee and I'm stuck in a car. It's hot and I'm hungry and you laugh at me? Still the bee kept trying to get out the rear window. Glass was glass, but eventually he would creep over a lip and buzz away.

The Lute Music CD

THE LUTE MUSIC CD remained on the phone table for five months though they didn't have a phone anymore. They didn't have children either and there were no substitutes.

His friend Paul had given the lute music CD to him as a birthday present. *Something different*, said the accompanying card. When dusting, she refused to dust the front cover displaying a Flemish print of a bleak country landscape. Even if some part of her happened to like lute music, the CD repelled her because he had ignored it so.

In bed at night she would look at his back. Sometimes he spoke in his sleep. I actually don't like you, Paul, he said, or, Try to get on top of me.

She wanted to start smoking so she could ash all over his naked, sweating body. She'd be more unhealthy, but a little happier. Things would even out or at least she'd hurt less and he'd hurt more.

The Iron

THE IRON CAME FROM a rummage sale. He said, Why not? Her mother had told her never to buy used appliances. She didn't love him too much anymore so she didn't argue.

He took little when he left her but the iron stayed behind, on a high shelf with an old *National Geographic,* its underside speckled with black dots, its dial set to linen.

She used to like to iron, but not now. She would come home after work, fix a drink, put on dance music, and sit down.

The iron hadn't moved in three months. He'd used it once when they went to an event at the university. It works really good, he'd called from the bathroom, holding the iron away from his body.

I hate you, she whispered.

WINTER'S DISJECTA

More Love

HE WANTED MORE LOVE, but his mother thought that was a bad idea. You don't want more, you want better love, she said. No, he said, more. So he drove to the clinic and filled out the forms. In the examination room the doctor injected him. They told him to sleep but he went to the beach and splashed in the water. A couple under an umbrella watched him. This is more love! he shouted. This is!

In his mother's house he took off his shirt. Look at all this more love! he said.

His mother sat, boiling eggs. Quietly she rose and tended to his sunburned neck. Her hand settled on his skin and his heat increased. She tightened her hold and he realized how she was hurting him. Better, she said.

Screws, Wall, and Him

After too long looking at silver screws he decided he wanted nice things. The silver screws were unevenly attached to his wall and they weren't even silver anymore—they were unhappy. And he was unhappy. He went to the store.

The first nice thing was a painting of a seaside—a pockmarked beach with no dead fish, only twigs. Optimistic painter, he thought, and he looked at those contained-looking, but maybe not contained, waves as they moved off the canvas and down the dirty wall to touch his feet. Waves touching his feet was a nice thing and he brightened at the beach on his wall—things as they were were nice again.

The second nice thing was a necklace not for neck but wall, and on wall it drooped its black and ivory beads while looking out at him, saying, Thank you for buying me; it's great to be on a wall with nice things. He nodded to the necklace, but his neck tightened and his hearing went away for a little while. Why wouldn't necklace want to be on neck? Why wouldn't neck want to have necklace? But he needed nice things in front of his eyes. Even the black beads, though dark, shed light.

With a few more screws to cover he went back for more but couldn't find any, so he returned home, happy to have at least a few nice things. He looked at them and they looked at him. All three giving a little to make the relationship work.

After dinner he thought he heard the painting ask if he himself was a nice thing and he said, Of course I am—it takes a nice thing to know other nice things. How could you ever not think I was a nice thing? I don't know, it said, I've been looking you over for a week or so and I think maybe sometimes you are and sometimes you aren't.

This hurt. How could this nice thing say such a thing? He didn't know. How could he answer when being a nice thing himself precluded him from saying bad things? And that painting, that voice behind the painting, if it was such a nice thing, what was it doing saying bad things? The ocean was okay, but nice? He was going to give the painting one more chance, but didn't and took it away, leaving one nice thing.

The necklace was quieter, more gentle. He'd liked its attitude from the start. The beads didn't pretend to move, just kept centered, content, ready to embrace the most vicious the world had to offer.

And he ate in comfort, the beaded necklace keeping steady, very steady, so steady he became a little concerned. He knew it was a necklace, but why didn't it move, why didn't it say something to him, like, Good job baking that pie? It wasn't about good or pie; it was him in front of a wall. Why was the necklace just drooping there? He looked at it up close, ran his thumb over the beads both black and white and said, Does this tickle? Does this make you feel anything? His necklace had gone numb, beads too stolid to be surprised with joy. Such a thing could not be nice. And since he had become a nice thing he had to surround himself only with nice things, necklace not one of them.

He slept for a few hours before he went back in front of the wall. Screws, wall, and him. The screws weren't so bad. Maybe they weren't nice, but they didn't pretend to be anything other than they were—they were screws. And the wall couldn't improve itself—it did its job. Screws, wall, and him—a nice slogan. And him—he kept it all together. The idea man of the three. A nice man with many ideas.

Or So

WHEN THEY HAD SEX AGAIN, somewhere near the end—because his throttling was extra sensory after she'd been three months without another man and because she was near to breaking into blossom—she said, Oonooo. Or so she thinks. But she is right. She knows what she said because she remembers everything, even the bad things—especially the bad things. It wasn't that this was a bad thing or that he was a bad thing, it was just that orgasm with someone she didn't really love anymore brought disturbance. This would have to be the last. She had to get on with her life, but even more, he had to get on. He should take piano lessons or read some Buddha, but he seriously had to leave her alone.

WHEN THEY HAD SEX AGAIN, somewhere in the middle, she told him she loved him, though it came out garbled as, Ioveooo. Or so he thinks. It made him happy and he instantly called what they were doing love-making, not acid-refucks. The rest of their time conjoined felt spectacular, a new beginning. They were alive with love. His doubts ceased and just before their orgasms he planned an itinerary for their once-postponed Southwest trip. He'd even buy the more expensive digital camera. Now that they were having sex again, he'd be fitter, more attractive without a shirt.

The Beige Futon

He went back into the moments when he'd create jagged sutures of kisses on her paralyzed arms and she'd murmur how she'd love him forever. But those moments blurred as another attacked—her saying she'd love him forever, though she left him for someone more secure and less in his head.

Sitting on the subway, he laughed aloud and a man with a picture of a taco on his shirt didn't seem too happy, and he thought, Why can't I laugh on the subway? The one time I do, a massive soft shell of guilt envelops me? So he closed his eyes and went back to the first moments, but those had changed. He was alone with their futon and it was dark and rainy. In reality the futon no longer existed—it had been taken to the dump months before, though it was still a good bed, it served its purpose, and he opened an eye to see the digital readout of stations overhead because maybe he'd reverse course and head to the dump. Hey guys, hi, there's a beige futon I brought here on the weekend of October 11th–12th or 12th–13th, I can't remember, but I remember the dumpster—green dumpster, many fluorescent lights, with a smelly couch. Any idea? And then he walked toward the green dumpster dressed in khakis, his least favorite pants, and he put his lips together on the subway in a dissonant pucker and the taco-shirted guy became extremely not happy because the pucker could easily arc up in the air and fall onto his hetero lips. He didn't want any part of a man's kiss—he worked for a living, drank in the evening, and he wanted a woman with a fiesta-sorta butt, not a thin though clean-shaven dude with a heavy book on his lap, a pinkie trapped inside. Yet the pucker continued and grew juicy because the originator of the pucker couldn't control his daydream wardrobe, the ends of his khakis getting sooty as he walked to the green dumpster. Dreams were tough, but they could be easy too, as amazingly they found the green dumpster that held the beige futon and the head of the crew gave him his personal truck so he could take the beige futon home, but to where? They didn't live there anymore. He lived in Bay Ridge and she lived in a place where he couldn't find her. His pinkie really hurt. These dreams of you, he wondered, but which you? Him? Her? The pucker soon broke and the taco-shirted man relaxed.

Mother

I CALLED MY MOTHER to tell her I wasn't feeling so good about my life and she told me to join the club, but this didn't sound right to me because I was already in the club, and I asked if she wanted to join my club. No, she wasn't interested because she was already in the club, and I asked how she knew she was already in it, and she said she wasn't going to talk to me about that stuff, and I said I didn't appreciate that, and she said, Tough.

Then I didn't know what to say. She asked if I was all right, and I said, No, I'm not all right, I told you before. I'm not feeling so good about my life. Your life? she asked. Yes, I said, and she said, What does that mean? I said, I didn't know what my life meant and maybe that was the problem. But that's not a problem, she said, nobody knows what their life means. Yes, everyone has the same problem. Exactly, she said, if everyone has the same problem, it's not really a problem. You're wrong, I said. Your mother is not wrong. This time you are, I said. There is no this time, she said. You don't believe in the present moment? I said. I don't believe in anything that makes me unhappy. I wish I had your powers, I said. They aren't powers, she said. And you should be able to access this way of thinking because I created you.

I don't want to access that way of thinking, I said. I believe in the power of unhappiness.

I believe you aren't my son, she said.

After the End

SHE TOLD HIM her new boyfriend made her laugh and that she hadn't laughed in she didn't know how long. And he said, No-one can make you laugh without you giving them permission, and she said the new boyfriend had her permission eternally, and he asked if he had gained the permission before the laugh. What laugh? she asked. The initial laugh, he said, because any permission granted thereafter would not count. I hate you, she said. And I hate stories about how you laugh, he said. But my hatred is more meaningful, she said, because I hate your entire person, your entire history, even our years together, whereas you only hate a story that contains a man you've had to tell yourself you hate. Then you hate yourself, he said. I used to hate myself because I was with you, she said, but now that I'm not, I've forgiven myself. Then how can you hate our time together? he asked. I hate our time together because it is symbolic of everything I used to hate about myself—a hate that will never disappear, not with forgiveness or holy water, she said, and he didn't say anything because he wanted her to say more, but she didn't, and he offered her a piece of gum and she accepted. I'm glad you still like gum, he said. Oh yeah, gum I could never hate. Maybe we should have chewed more gum, he said. No, then I would hate gum too. But you just said you could never hate gum. That was before gum and you started to have a close relationship. I think I'm growing to hate you too, he said. Yes, she said, don't you see how fun this is?

DESCANT

She Told the Man,
the Man Told Me

YESTERDAY, at the café on that busy boulevard, I wrote a notation concerning my feelings for the people in this world. I started writing the notation on a page in my workbook, but I felt the words too trite, so I crossed them out and rewrote in the margins of a cookbook abandoned on the small silver table holding milk and sweeteners.

An older man walked into the café while I rewrote. He stared at me and the cookbook before coughing and going to the counter. I again crossed out the notation and checked the quality of my pen against the surface of the table before inking there. This rewriting of the notation took more time than I had conceived because I kept adding things. While the notation itself was sound, below it I had to explain a little more so anyone reading it might understand the frightened words it held. And I was lucky to have the table because at times my penmanship ballooned and I needed a large space to contain myself.

On the table I told of a woman friend of a friend and her troubled past weeks. It started when she was hit by a car—luckily, a glancing blow. The driver left the scene, and as it happened early on a Sunday morning, when most people slept, she had no-one to console her. She went to the hospital, but they told her she was fine. There's nothing wrong with me? she asked the nurses. No, nothing. This woman went home and called her sister. As she told her sister about the accident, the woman fell down the steps of her duplex. The sister wanted to know what had happened and she told her she'd had another accident and had just fallen down the steps. The woman went back to the hospital. Everything is hurting, she told them. Everything about me hurts. They examined her and told her it wasn't that bad and she probably hadn't needed to come to the hospital. Since her doctor was closed on Sundays, they could understand how she wanted to come to them, even though some people in her situation might not have bothered. Then they released her.

This woman went home and put on some chamber music—an album she hadn't listened to in a while. The music, how it was interpreted and played, reminded her how moments in life could also be finely tuned. As the pieces swept aside her anxiety, she drank tea. When she walked into the kitchen to get more hot water, the limp she thought she had from the fall was not there. Tea and violins, tea and calm.

As the sky darkened, she began lighting candles for the appearance of her lover, a man white-haired and often lonely who used to belong to a radical political group. Lately, he had been overseas investigating a son in trouble, but he had returned, speaking proudly of the pie he would bake and bring her that evening. Yet this lover, this man, did not arrive at the appointed time or after, and the woman sunk into oblivion on her most cherished sofa, a five-year-old cranberry affair, a gift from her estranged father.

He has met someone else. He has grown tired of me. My body cannot charm him. These thoughts made up the rest of her evening, and, in between bouts of weeping, she pulled the covers from her bed and slept on the sofa.

The light in the morning was diffuse. A team of surveyors in bright orange uniforms had set up on her street and were talking loudly and laughing loudly. She closed her windows but could still hear them. They spoke their words in a thoughtlessly happy fashion, laughing the laugh of forgetfulness while making money.

She left the house.

The subway was crowded and she took the paperback she had finished last week out of her purse and began reading from the beginning. A mystery set in Lisbon with an element of romance. On the first read through she'd realized how badly written the book was, but this time it was painful. She closed it and stared at the list of coming stations on that line. She would travel to the end, stretching the system as far as it could go—she thought doing so would stop her mind. Along the way she concentrated on sounds: wheels on the tracks, the blowing of air vents, the tinny crashing of music from the headphones of a boy beside her. When she opened her eyes they seized on people's shoes and the various conditions of the footwear. She had never consciously grasped how many different types existed. How many colors they came in. How at home patches of dirt seemed on some. How some had no laces and some had too many.

It continued on, this volley of sensory attentions in a world that had fooled her too many times. Soon, a couple of men in cowboy boots stepped on—both pairs brown, worn, and scuffed. The men did not sit. They had guitars. As soon as the doors closed, a storm of mariachi music began. It was as loud as music could be on the subway, and though the men sang with smiles, and though the music broadcast was cheerful and, if the phrases could be translated, probably joyful and promising, her stomach rose on alert and a terrific terror pinned her being. The men seemed to grow emboldened and inexplicably increased the volume of their instruments. Frozen, she endured for a moment, but soon a heat circled her ears. Putting her hands to them only made them hotter. Her arms fell to her sides and she tipped her torso, too sick to be straight. She stopped the tipping but was sure blood would run from her ears. The song continued, the longest song in the largest space between stations in the system. How could it have happened this way? The man not singing grinned at her, his broken teeth glazed with spit. Though she kept her face closed to his happiness, something cracked inside her. She curled her wrists and coughed hard not to feel the cracking, but she did, nothing could stop it. She opened her mouth for her own sounds to comfort her but she couldn't produce them. The men's thick fingers slapped at their guitars, and for the first time she could remember, she had no light in her life.

After the train stopped, she staggered off and went up the stairs into the cloudy morning. Near the edge of the city, she soon came upon a park with a large lagoon. At its edge she examined the green twisting water with flecks of leaves and twigs. She startled as test sirens went off in the distance, and looked to others walking nearby. They seemed to know to ignore it. When she returned to the water, it remained much the same. Folding and unfolding forms of muddied time. Look at it all, so simple, so wise— the earth peed this.

She sat by the bank. After the sirens died she couldn't hear any noise except the momentary flick of her tongue trying to talk, but who would receive her speech? The grass under her hands smelled rained upon. The cold lagoon water shifting in and out of cold and in and out of warm. She was incredibly alone.

Later, she walked by the boathouse, an off-white structure with peeling paint. More and more people were coming to this large building, entering the snack bar or knocking on the rental office windows. The canoes and kayaks were now ready to use. Maybe there would be sun. She crept onto the narrow pier, often looking back as she proceeded, then glancing from side to side at the green water.

Back on land she watched a father and son walking on the macadam path ringing the lagoon. Something had just happened between them because their heads were down and they walked slowly. She followed, having to make sure they were safe. The father was fairly young and fairly athletic, his shirt tight against his chest. His son had messy blond hair and a pale face. They were kind people, they'd lived a completely different life from her, but now they had a vanquished air. Such sadness would soon disappear. It couldn't last long, with children it never did, or so she was told, and so she remembered, though she remembered wrongly. Sadness did stay with children. It stayed with them their whole lives.

The father walked to the edge of the path and took off his pack. The water bottle he handled was silver and blue. The boy shook his offer away and the man drank, a short sip. Then the boy clapped his cheeks before quickly facing in her direction, as if he'd known she'd been there. She couldn't turn from him because the rest of her life depended on what he'd do next. Though the boy didn't understand much, he could understand trouble and forgot her, walking closer to his father, closer and closer before he fell into the man—rubbing his way into a hold, laughing or crying at reunion, she couldn't tell which.

Walking away, she dismissed what she'd witnessed. What other people did couldn't matter to her. She had made it this far in life. One day she would meet someone special.

When I stepped away from the table, I felt a certain pleasure I'd known only a few times in life. I scanned my work, finding all the paragraph breaks and spellings to be sound. Not a single mistake in that thing.

Descant

THIS COUPLE, THEN, entered, without their knowing it, an unendurable zone, years in the making. Most nights they came back to their apartment in Greenpoint from their office jobs, though he returned thirty minutes before her. Then they ate, often take-out, and watched TV, often the latest cutting-edge series. It's not that they didn't speak, but they weren't exactly thrilled to hear each other. They created a stagey type of interplay, with a lessening of surprises, so that everything was gists and gestures—the pretense often indicating the expected. Seven years they'd logged, five together, and they moved to Greenpoint just when the cool people left it, bemoaning the fact that their few important friends, who all lived in Brooklyn, rarely made the ponderous trip via the homunculus of the subway, the G.

That summer he waited in dread, but he wasn't ready to relinquish the life they shared, to believe another human had been made who understood him as well as her, who smelled as sweetly. These were the thirty sweatiest and most beautiful minutes of his day, as he sat quietly, listening to his neighbor's intricate sound system which registered the thumping music for a videogame he'd been playing for nearly two years. What if she didn't come home? What if this was finally the day she decided to leave, though most break-ups happened on the weekend due to working people's greater proximity? What if she died? Why would a thirty-five-year-old have a will?

Masturbating didn't help him, though the time would have been sufficient to fantasize, mount himself by hand, and yank at his preferred speed. He continued to do what he had done most of the day at work, often when no-one important was looking on—focus on his feed and watch what everyone else was doing with their lives. At least someone had fun. Though even there people had taken to proclaiming their dissatisfactions, at the expense of making fools of themselves. One old depressed friend, who they rarely saw anymore because their depressions made a mad misshapen triangle, had just posted a picture of a door lying on the grass in Prospect Park with the caption: *I saw this door on the grass and thought there would be a better, kinder world behind it. I went to open it, but it was locked.* Still, he continued to search for something, some testimony, alacrity, even grandeur or scorn. He became envious of people who lived alone.

Nietzsche once groused, If you aren't attracted to someone's deficiencies during the courting phase of a relationship, a proper base for the future would be lacking. For the last year, telling each other they were tired beat out *I love you* by a ratio of four-to-one. They still did things together: Governor's Island in the summer, a bike ride, an art exhibit, a Scrabble party in Bushwick that happened less and less. The weekends were a special problem they solved by sleeping late and running errands alone, though she mostly preferred the latter course, leaving him little choice. So how did it work at all? They were each attracted to someone with similar interests, who lived in New York ironically, that is tendentiously, and who knew what *attenuated* meant. Yet they didn't fall in love with what one another represented so much as they latched onto a means of escape from the lonely weekend hours of seeing couples suck face and those interminable bar nights enduring unhappy, borderline alcoholics who pretended to be charming, to have read deeper meanings into Dostoevsky.

That they were a sort of bookish intellectual couple, with the usual left leanings, was another cog in their disintegration—*inhibited* being the watchword for a retrograde course in their communication. They quietly read their books and rarely discussed them, an attitude breeding no learning and no desire, except to say they should check out a specific article in the weekend paper. She liked to read the great shorter works of sociology and philosophy, while he enjoyed contemporary non-fiction—books about food, the mind, and social injustice.

She liked to walk and as she walked to work alone she remembered how she used to walk alone almost all the time before she met him. She missed those days, when she freely decided what she would do and for how long—a strange magic she had taken for granted. She had a perpetual duck mouth and large brown glasses often settling low on her nose, making her small blue eyes smaller. She wouldn't begin conversations with him but just react to what he said, like she played baby to his adult. Inside, things were quite different. We never take pictures together, she reminded herself, as though the wounded side of her brain would have forgotten. Of course you wouldn't forget, the masochistic side said (she had more than two sides), I'm trying to make you angry so you move on now and don't break out into violence later. Yes, she said sadly, We don't take pictures because we don't want to be reminded of these times, these years, our thirties, when seemingly normal people start to pull it together and realize life can be put in some order, just keep the money flowing. As she read of logic and societal changes atop the widening disappointment of her life, she tried to register the turmoil with a stony face, but a patch of pale skin on her right cheek turned more and more puce, her only tell.

By the afternoon of Saturday or Sunday, when they had usually been away from each other for hours, the draw to be around the familiar, however painful, rose up like a false alarm they nonetheless obeyed out of the annals of the co-dependency on which they unwittingly shared writing credit. They'd go to the small café near their house because it was small, not many other people could fit inside, let alone see them. The baristas, following the owner's fashion, often played classical music, giving it a much different ambiance than most places, a kind of liberal library feel, where many patrons read printed material and electronic articles while Bach, Beethoven, and Dvořák graced their ears. On a Sunday in May, he arrived ahead of her and tried to read as a woman and her friend talked loudly, while the child of one ran about and banged its head against the glass door. He gave up giving them judgmental looks after ten minutes, though he'd been reading the same paragraph for five while his mind raced to the moment of his lady joining him and how it would of course be about the same as always. She'd buy her own coffee, even though he offered to get it, and then she'd immediately pull out her book and not pay much mind except for correcting him when he misidentified the composer of the old music they heard.

Just after she arrived, the two women with the baby left and he breathed freely, but in a disturbed way, thinking their loudness a CIA-sanctioned torture that would have brought her closer to him through their exchange of pissy looks—yes, they still had that brand of sangfroid. But then, too, the baby would be there, jeering at their agreed upon barrenness with all those messy/cute baby qualities, incapable of being inculcated by their selfish morality. As she stood in the line for her macchiato, he noted the jungle green shirt she wore—a favorite of his, though they'd stopped that talk a few years ago. She appeared even thinner, like she'd donated her hips to charity, and he tugged at his beard, staring angrily at the words in his book. She came back and slid out her pamphlet-sized discourse on belief. He broke open a chocolate bar he'd bought before he came to the café and offered it. She didn't see it for thirty seconds or pretended not to, though he held it at eye level about four inches from her face. Then, slowly, she took it without looking up from her book. She bit into it, and said, Thank you, while chewing and reading. Maybe this was the moment, he thought. Begin it here. *I've been doing some thinking...* No, that triteness wasn't worthy of them, no matter how fucked up they were, let them keep some dignity. Or he could say something more parabolic—a story of how they used to be and how it wasn't feasible anymore. No, even with Mozart on, especially with Mozart on, no. They should confine their mess to the apartment and not contaminate Greenpoint any further. Then, for some minutes, he brightened. He actually liked what they did and how they could sit soundlessly reading next to each other, being with someone who was trusted enough not to require pointless gabbing, and he focused on her, happy and hopeful, until it easily vanished like the lie it was. He again became a dog in want of love or at least a look—acknowledgement. She could have given him that. No, it was all wrong. Trust could mean so little.

She knew when someone looked at her from fifty yards away in a crowded concert. Just do it, he gave you chocolate. No, she cried and the dull baseline pain sharpened and she struggled not to move in co-operation. He must not win. He must think it's all his fault. Which was certainly not true, but he would continue beating up on himself, he carried that from childhood—she could not hold his hand forever. Why be too big to go to therapy? Start ending the suffering. She'd told him enough. What the hell? She'd not look. But her bookmark, which her thumb kept on the opposing page of the one she read, fell to the ground. Fuck. Now she'd have to pick it up, unless the woman of the couple who'd just sat down next to them would. That woman (who of course wouldn't let her own boyfriend—Indian, cute—sit next to another woman) didn't.

She kept herself turned from her, but also askew from her man—
pretzeled and holding an odd energy.

Perturbed, she leaned down to pick up the bookmark, which
advertised an out-of-business bookstore in Connecticut she'd enjoyed in her youth. Then she continued reading, curling her lip at
the sentence *Not to be absolutely certain is, I think, one of the essen-
tial things in rationality*, and as she continued reading she came
to feel, and then to notice, that the couple at the next table, who
hadn't said anything but just sat with their drinks, were now
looking at the two of them in a vague way. And she noticed that
he, who chewed chocolate, was glancing pityingly across to a bulle-
tin board on the wall which, beneath a sheet detailing Persian
lessons, displayed an ad for the Frick with a painting of a woman
whose arch, sidelong glance mocked them all—even a person
four hundred years dead could see how unhappy they were. But
the other couple, maybe five years younger, continued to dwell as
listlessly as before, until the woman suddenly pivoted and spoke
to her man. You have no respect for me, she said in an even tone
but a voice loud enough to be openly audible. As he replied, the
speakers projected the slow movement of a symphony.

Oh yeah? See, the thing is I don't respect liars.

I lied to protect you.

He bristled. To protect yourself—and you were still stupid
enough to tell the wrong person and get caught.

Not here, she said, and she gestured.

On the street? So I don't embarrass you? You started it.

You can't help embarrassing me, you sad piece of shit. You
live for it.

He laughed. Yes, I live for this. He grabbed the back of her neck
and jerked her up. Let's go, Cheri. Something I want to show you,
Cheri. She cried feebly and grabbed at the front of his pants, but

he brushed her hand away and whispered, *fuckyou fuckyou fuckyou*, as he propelled her out the door.

They sat stunned. They both glanced at the barista, who unwrinkled her forehead and went back to the dishes. Sick, he slowly wrapped up the uneaten chocolate.

They continued to look at their books, but now they didn't read. She didn't want to leave because she didn't want to see the other couple flailing outside, no doubt marooned and not moving. After ten minutes of silence, he stood, knowing her well enough to know she wanted to go. In a reversal, she waited for him while he put on his coat more slowly, instead of rushing outside as usual. But that would be the last consideration she exercised before leaving the apartment for a friend's house that night. Don't go, some voice inside him wanted to cry out, just like in a movie or TV show. They hadn't finished the fifth season of the show they had simultaneously judged as the fourth-best of all time. There was only one episode left. But he could do that alone. There was some kind of life in TV if everyone watched it.

Acknowledgements

The following stories have appeared previously, all in much different form: 'Manhattan' (one) in *Juked*; 'Chrissy Likes the Dolphins,' 'Overtone,' 'Reviewed,' 'My Bed-Stuy Friend,' 'The Bookcase,' and 'The Bee' in *elimae*; 'I Might Be Here in February' in *Quarterly West*; 'High on the Thigh' and 'Three Rich Women' in *The Collagist*; 'Here Is the Poem,' 'Lyrically,' and 'My Unhappy Writer Friend' in *Puerto del Sol*; 'They Do Not Complete Me' in *LIT*; 'Issues' in *Nano Fiction*; 'Telling' and 'The Shirt' in *PANK*; 'The Lute Music CD' in *Denver Quarterly*; 'The Iron' in *matchbook*; 'More Love' in *Quick Fiction*; 'Or So' in *Broken Pencil*; 'The Beige Futon' in *Word Riot*; 'Mother' in *Everyday Genius*; and 'Descant' in *Columbia Journal*.

SPLICE

ThisIsSplice.co.uk

www.ingramcontent.com/pod-product-compliance
Lightning Source LLC
Chambersburg PA
CBHW030641190726
48286CB00008B/2606